McKensie Stewart

An
Emily Graham
Novel

Tillman Publishing

Shattered
An Emily Graham Novel
All Rights Reserved.
Copyright © 2017 McKensie Stewart
v2.0 r1.0

Paperback ISBN: 978-0-578-18570-5
Hardback ISBN: 978-0-578-18571-2

Library of Congress Control Number: 2016956974

Cover Photo © 2017 thinkstockphotos.com. All rights reserved - used with permission.

Tillman Publishing

PRINTED IN THE UNITED STATES OF AMERICA

Chapter 1

*E*mily bolts straight up from a deep slumber. The sleeping pills she took the night before allowed her to relax her restless mind and body and combat her insomnia. But sleep hasn't come easy for Emily over the last six months; her battle to regain control of her life has caused her to toss and turn wondering how to be "happy" again. She looks around the room and sighs as she catches a glimpse of the dark circles around her eyes and the patches of silver at her temples. Emily's thoughts take her away from her stagnant relationship with Brendon, back to the person who she should have married. Why did she let societal pressure lead her to walk away from true love and run towards what felt acceptable and safe? "Acceptable and safe for whom?" Is it safe to wander lost with a heart that never mends?

Emily closes her eyes and massages her temples; her head starts to hurt as she opens and closes her mouth wide to relieve the tension in her jaw. "Ouch." Her jaw pops once and then again as she stretches away its stiffness. She opens her eyes mechanically, and slowly turns her attention towards the window, then glances around the room at the overstuffed, pricey furniture. This room, especially, makes Emily's stomach churn. It looks and feels like Brendon's mother, Kyndall: pretentious and bourgeois. After all these years, Emily still finds it creepy that Kyndall wanted to decorate their bedroom, which was the stipulation of her giving them the down payment to their $500,000 house. Emily shudders at the memory of them sitting in the attorney's office on that day in July.

Even though it was sweltering outside, she was cold. She had brought a jacket to cover the sleeveless, floral dress she decided to wear. Brendon and she were holding hands, excited to be purchasing their first house together, even though they knew the type of control they would have to endure from Kyndall if they accepted her offer. Emily was young, and thought she would be too busy with work and a family to let Kyndall's dominance intimidate her…but she was clearly wrong. Kyndall was in rare form; she was overjoyed that Brendon and Emily would be living down the block from her and Wellington. Society Hill was a quiet street that would put them within distance to rub elbows with the elite in Philadelphia. Kyndall made sure of that. She gave Brendon's hand a little squeeze, "My Brendon will only have the best. You will one day be President of the United States and need to establish your presence with the right people by living among those who can help your career advance." She patted his hand one last time. "Take my lead and you will go far."

Kyndall turned her head toward the right, where her husband, Wellington Graham, the attorney general, was sitting. "At least I will be able to groom *one* of the men in my life to aspire to greatness. You know I wanted you to be President, but that's okay. I have my Brendon to rely on to pave this family's way to the White House. I deserve the White House," Kyndall exclaimed.

Even though the comment was designed to be heard only by Wellington, Kyndall's shrill voice echoed throughout the office. Her husband's breathing started to get short and choppy; his knuckles turned white as he gripped the end of the armchair. He jumped and exited the room in haste, slamming the door behind him.

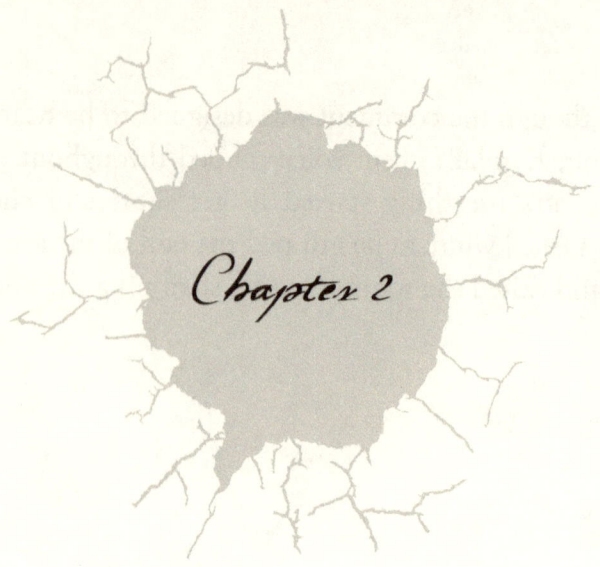

The admiration and pride Kyndall has for Brendon stems from her humble beginnings in West Philly. Kyndall's father, Patrick Sullivan, worked as a groundskeeper at Philadelphia General Hospital. Her mother, Alice, worked in the cafeteria, washing dishes. Kyndall's family was poverty-stricken but always kept their hand-me-down clothes clean and held their heads high as they walked down the street to church every Sunday morning. Each morning before school, Alice lectured Kyndall on believing in herself and knowing her self-worth wasn't measured in dollars but in love from family and helping those less fortunate. "Look them square in the eye and never hold your head down because you will be the person you aspire to be. One day you will have nice clothes and marry a strong, educated man who will care for you. This is where your training begins to show how important you are in the world. Remember, you are just as good as the others." Kyndall heard Alice's speech everyday and knew it inside and out.

At first it was hard for Kyndall to accept what her mother

was saying because her clothes were tattered and threadbare and the girls at school had clothes that were new and not as faded as hers. Kyndall's shoes had a hole in the bottom and her father inserted a piece of cardboard the length of her shoe to shield her feet from debris. She was especially careful not to step in water puddles when it rained because the water soaked through the cardboard, leaving Kyndall's feet wet and, in the winter, cold with the tips of her toes purple from the dampness of the snow. Kyndall liked when there were heavy downpours because she could wear her shiny black shoes that she was otherwise allowed to wear only for church and special occasions. She took pride in keeping them clean with the tiny cloth she used to shine her shoes. She mimicked her father, as he shined his boots with a similar cloth.

Patrick was a very pensive man. He stopped shining his shoes and dropped the cleaning cloth before inspecting his work. He carefully took the right shoe and looked it over with a smile. He then gently put the right boot on the floor and reached for the left. He glanced over the left boot and brushed a speckle of sand away. Kyndall remembered wondering if the lonely piece of sand was imaginary... Patrick never left any dirt behind.

One day, as Kyndall marveled at this small ceremony, she drummed up the courage to ask, "Why do you shine your old work boots? They are old and there's a hole in the right boot and a part of your big toe sticks out. Why put so much care in something so old that needs to be thrown in the trash?"

The inspection carried on for ten minutes before Patrick cleared his throat and replied, "If we don't appreciate what the Lord has given us, He may not bless us in the future. You should show that you are thankful for what He has given us. Never take anything that He does for you for granted."

Kyndall looked up at her father with wide, sheepish eyes and responded, "Yes, father." She locked these words up in the depths of her heart and did her best to live them, until his death.

After Patrick's death, Alice raised Kyndall as a single parent while still working at the hospital. Alice was a strong woman. Although she pretended to scoff, secretly she admired the students who came through the nursing program. She enjoyed listening to their stories of where they came from and their dreams for the future. Even though many of the nursing students were from affluent families, they specially came to Philadelphia General Hospital to care for the indigent in the inner city. They wanted the world to be a better place and knew that their hard work would positively impact those who needed their service the most.

Alice knew that she wanted her daughter to have more than she had growing up, and wanted Kyndall to marry someone who could care for her, give her a better life with fancy clothes and perfume. She remembered one of the nursing students coming through the cafeteria smelling like roses. The smell made her dream of running through a field, arms floating through the air, wearing a sheer dress and matching scarf that fluttered in the breeze as she twirled among the bluebells. She felt light enough to take flight. The smells made her want to be carefree and imagine a life for her daughter without boundaries, without restrictions. It was too late for her, but her daughter needed a better life, one she could never offer her.

That same nursing student would purposefully be the last to eat in the cafeteria to strike up conversation with Alice on various scholarship opportunities to fund Kyndall's education. Alice may not have had the best education, but she would follow the student's advice on how to get Kyndall into Temple. Each afternoon, Alice would compile her notes and work on her strategy. Alice's hard work and determination helped Kyndall become recognized as a scholar. She was admitted to the university with a scholarship that paid for her entire four-year education.

To this day, Kyndall gives thanks to her parents for the hard life lessons, and knows without them, her legacy at Temple would not exist. She serves the university as a member of the board of trustees and wears the title with great pride.

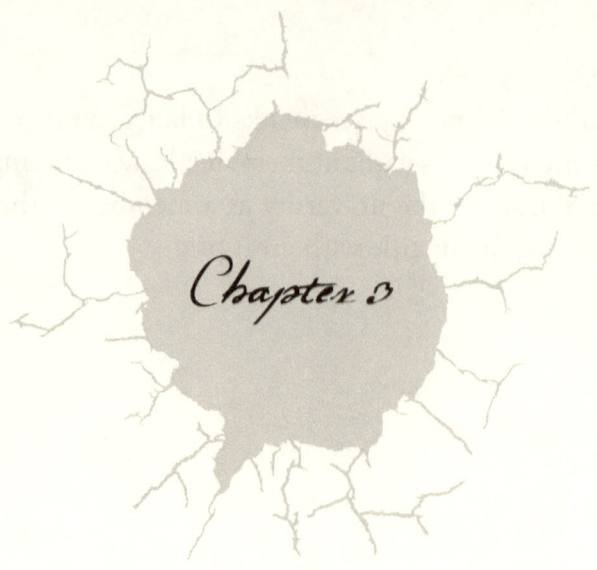

Chapter 3

*T*he alarm clock sounds and reminds Emily how distasteful she finds sleeping through her life. Today is the day that she will wake and face her dysfunctional marriage, life, and husband, Brendon Graham, senator for the State of Pennsylvania. Emily tosses the covers back and immediately starts for the scarf drawer in her walk-in closet. She pulls out a manila, legal-sized envelope, moving her fingers across the metal clasps to fold them in to open it. Emily reaches in and pulls out the divorce documents that she asked her attorney to draw up months ago, but never had the courage to speak with Brendon about. Brendon's hectic schedule provided the perfect excuse to delay the conversation. He works between DC and Philadelphia, leaves on Monday and comes home to his family in Pennsylvania on Friday. His schedule is like clockwork: take the 5:00 a.m. Northeast Regional Amtrak train from 30th Street Station in Philadelphia, which arrives at 7:00 a.m. in DC, leaves the capital on the Acela Express train, and arrives by 8:32 p.m. in Philadelphia.

Brendon called last evening to tell Emily that he and his staff would be working late to put the finishing touches on a bill that he would introduce to Congress on Monday, which was the first bill that he was sponsoring for his state. He needed to get the support at this point from the north, south, east, and west and would be home Saturday evening. Emily said, "Okay, but when you come home on Saturday evening, the two of us need to talk. There is so much we need to catch up with."

Brendon said, "I love you," but Emily didn't answer. She had already taken the phone away from her ear and ended the call.

The knock on the bedroom door startles Emily, and she drops the divorce papers on the closet floor. She yells, "Coming" as she kneels and gathers up the papers into the semblance of a pile.

In her frenzy, she shoves the manila envelope haphazardly into the dresser. She doesn't notice the corner of the papers peeking out from the partially closed drawer. As Emily exits the closet, she reaches for the robe hanging on the back of the door. She struggles to get her arms through as she scurries toward the door. She opens the bedroom door and sees two adorable children on the other side: Madison and Connor, her eight-year-old fraternal twins.

Madison asks, "Are you taking us to school today?"

Emily quickly looks at her Rolex and shouts, "Shoot! Did you have breakfast?"

Madison responded, "Yes."

Emily breathes a sigh of relief; thank God for Ms. Pearl.

Ms. Pearl has been the backbone of the Graham family and Emily's most trusted confidant since before the children were born. Even then, she supported the daily and weekly cleaning and the endless entertaining they did monthly. The dinner parties were designed to persuade and cajole colleagues in Congress; they drained Emily emotionally. Emily was never sure if Brendon's heart was in his mother's dream for him, but he showed up and played his part, regardless.

Ms. Pearl started working as the Grahams' housekeeper two weeks after she retired as a schoolteacher and graduated her last foster child. Foster children had a special place in her heart because she knew what it was like to grow up without a place she could call home. Henry, Pearl's father, shot himself and her mother, Mary Margaret, in a drunken rage. Pearl could never get that image out of her head, no matter how hard she tried.

She had heard the argument from her bedroom, which was nothing unusual, but her mother's voice seemed desperate as she pleaded with Henry not to strike her as he did several times a week. Henry worked Monday through Friday, and on Friday, he rushed over to the corner ABC Spirits store to cash his check and buy liquor. Henry's drink of choice was Johnnie Walker straight; no chaser, from the bottle, no glass or cup. Henry had been drinking all afternoon on that Friday. He paced the floor in the living room, waiting for Mary Margaret to come home. The key started to turn in the front door, unlocking the bolt. Henry heard Mary Margaret entering the house and greeted her in the living room.

Henry yelled, "I want my dinner on the table at 6:30! Where were you, with Mr. Barnes at Gus's Meat Market?"

Henry's rage seemed to be coming from a place where he couldn't understand what was real or made up in his mind. The alcohol clouded his judgment, and his accusations were deep and dark. He was seeing past Mary Margaret and answering to the demon that was pulling his strings to be ruthless to his devoted wife and mother of his child. Henry's vision became blurry. There were two Mary Margaret's in his view. He just needed to raise the gun and shoot the impostor. He started to stumble back and forth as he pointed the gun at his target. He used his shirttail to wipe the sweat from his eyes and forehead and blinked as perspiration dripped into his eyes and they began to sting. The voices came from every direction, and four images of Mary Margaret appeared before him.

"Henry, put the gun down," yelled Mary Margaret.

Henry shouted, "Make it stop, make it go away!"

He staggered forward, reaching for the sofa to regain his balance, and pointed the gun at the real Mary Margaret.

"Henry, no! Put down the gun! I promise dinner won't be late again! I will train Pearl to only use the bathroom at home and not when we are out. I just had so many bags and Pearl had to go," Mary Margaret screamed at the top of her lungs.

The next sound was the bang of the gun that rang throughout the house. *Thump* was the sound Pearl heard. Her mother spoke no more.

Pearl ran from her bedroom to the living room and she heard Henry. "Look what you made me do, Mary. Look what you made me do."

Bang. He, too, stopped talking after the loud bang and hard thump to the ground. Pearl stood stone still, staring at both her parents lying in a pool of their own blood. Finally, she sprang to action. She ran toward her mother's body and placed her head in her lifeless lap, unconcerned with the blood that stained her summer frock. She examined her mother's bloody hands, flipping them over not once but twice. Pearl gently caressed her mother's oval face and hair. "Mama, wake up; wake up, Mama!" Tears streamed down her face.

From her trance-like state, Pearl barely remembered Mrs. Martha, Mary Margaret's sister-in-law, running into the kitchen or the "Lord have mercy!" that echoed through the house as she ran to the kitchen to call the police. The police were on the scene in about five minutes. After they assessed the situation, they asked Mrs. Martha, "Is there family that can take Pearl? If not, she should go with social services for the night." Mrs. Martha explained, "I'm the only living relative that Pearl has, but I can't take Pearl, not even for one night."

She was embarrassed and couldn't tell the police the real

reason she didn't volunteer to take Pearl. Two years after Mary Margaret married Henry, the happy couple invited Martha to a blind date dinner with Henry's brother, Walter. It was love at first sight. Martha and Walter married six months later. It only took one month into the marriage for Walter to bust Martha's upper and lower lip for speaking when she wasn't spoken to in one of his drunken rages. Martha staggered over to Mary Margaret's home and rang the doorbell.

Mary Margaret came to the door, looked at Martha's face, and wailed, "I am so sorry, Martha." She started to cry. "I wasn't sure he was like that too."

That was when Martha knew that her best friend purposefully introduced her to a drunken wife abuser. The whole line of men in that family were drunks, from the great-great-grandfather who made moonshine to Walter's father, who hit his wife so hard that she lost two teeth during a fight. Mary Margaret reached out to comfort her, but Martha pulled away and walked home with her head down. She knew that she could never escape Walter's abuse because he declared that he would kill her before he would let her go.

Martha looked the police officer in the eye and told him, "Go ahead and call social services, because this child deserves a better life. My situation is no better than Mary Margaret's."

Martha slowly walked toward her home, shoulders drooping and feet dragging. She knew she did what was in Pearl's best interest; it would take a lifetime for her to get over what she had experienced, and Martha didn't want to add to her time in therapy due to Walter's wandering eye for the girl. Martha saw how Walter looked at Pearl and just didn't need that kind of trouble for herself or that little girl. Pearl would go on to do great things in the world and didn't need the scar of a drunken old man on top of her in the middle of the night.

Chapter 4

M s. Pearl appears out of nowhere. The sight of her oval face and plump figure makes Emily smile. Emily always thinks her as among the tallest women in the room, despite her height of five-foot-one. *She has a good heart,* Emily thinks. *I've never heard Pearl say anything nasty or negative about anyone. She has a soul in line with what our Heavenly Father intended for all of us.*

Emily never understood why Pearl did not have children, but knew she loved each one of her foster children as though they were her own. Emily hired Pearl because she was a stern disciplinarian with a kind heart, and knew one day when she and Brendon started their family they would need someone to keep the children in line and the house in order.

During the interview, Pearl boasted how each of her foster children went to either college or a trade school because she wanted them to have a brighter future than they had prior to meeting her. Emily hung onto Pearl's every word as they both laughed and got to know each other. The frank and open conversation with

Pearl made Emily start to think about how she missed her mother and needed to reach out to her.

Emily was in a trance as Pearl called Emily's name several times. "Mrs. Graham? Mrs. Graham? Mrs. Graham, are you okay?"

Emily focused her attention back on Pearl and then nervously looked around the room to see if Kyndall was lurking in the doorway or even behind her. "It's Emily, please call me Emily. Mrs. Graham is Brendon's mother's name. I would like you to call me Emily," Emily said with a smile on her face.

"Well then, Emily it is," Pearl said as she got up to leave. When Pearl and Emily walked to the door, Pearl said, "Mrs.... I mean Emily, are you okay? You seem a little distracted."

Emily's voice cracked and she took a deep breath. "I was listening to you talk about your foster children with so much love and admiration. I was missing my mother."

Pearl reached toward Emily and hugged her as though they had been friends for years. Emily received Pearl's hug and buried her head between Pearl's neck and shoulder.

"Baby, it's going to be okay. Go and call your mother or even surprise her with a visit. Your mother misses you just as much."

Emily lifted her head off Pearl's shoulder, taking in the sweet smell of jasmine. "Can you start tomorrow?"

"Well, all right, I will be here at seven to start breakfast. Breakfast is the most important meal of the day, and I see I need to put a little meat on those bones of yours." Pearl playfully swatted Emily on the butt.

Emily closed the door behind Pearl and headed to the bedroom to call her mother. She rummaged around the room and found her cell phone on the nightstand where she left it, hitting voice call from her contact list. "Hello?" came from the other end of the phone.

Emily started to cry. "Mother, I just called to tell you how much I love you. I don't tell you as much as I should."

The two of them talked for hours with Emily promising to visit soon.

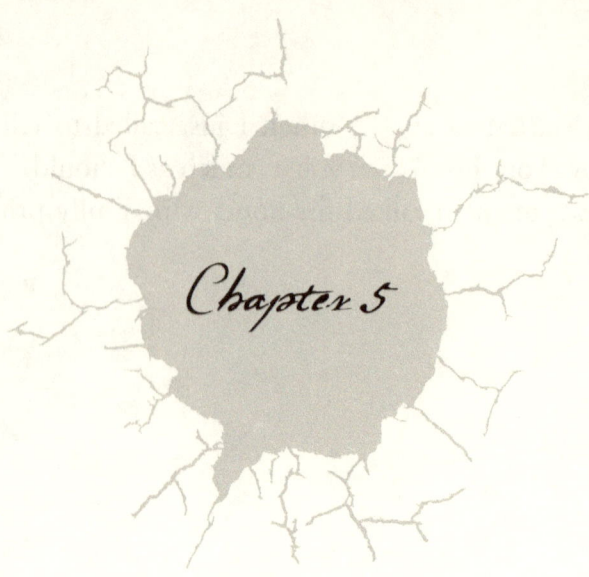

Chapter 5

Emily reaches for her keys and puts her purse on her shoulder. She yells for the children and they fall in line after their mother and head to the car. Pearl takes this quiet time to go to the grocery store to shop for dinner and leaves the house as well. Within minutes of everyone leaving, Kyndall pulls up and bangs the handle of the knocker against the white wood of the door. The resounding clatter conveys her disapproval at the idea of knocking on her son's door. Of knocking on the door of the house that she provided the down payment for; nevertheless, this was a "rule" that Emily gave Kyndall after she entered the home without notice on three occasions. *That bitch*, Kyndall thinks as she knocks a second time.

No one answers the door so Kyndall uses her spare key and unlocks the door. "Hello? Anyone home?" She looks in the kitchen and sees no one, then takes the stairs to the master suite and calls Emily's name while walking towards the closet. Again, no answer. Kyndall sees Emily's robe on the floor and walks towards the closet to hang it on the back of the closet door. The bits of paper poking out of the drawer catch her eye. Kyndall walks over and opens the drawer. In a flash, the manila envelope is in her hand; she plays with the clasps thinking that she should put the envelope back, but decides it is a better idea to open it. She moves with a quickness to close the closet door and pulls the papers out of the envelope.

Kyndall skims through all the pages of the divorce papers, citing the reason for the divorce as irreconcilable differences. *So, this is what the little bitch has been up to.* Kyndall recalls Emily's strange behavior over the last several months. She has chalked it up to the stress of being married to the senator and preparations for Brendon's run for the White House. *This family has come so far, and Emily will not crush our dreams by divorcing Brendon. The marriage was pieced together with bribes and threats, and Emily will not destroy what I have built.*

Brendon doesn't realize how much he needs her. Kyndall will suggest that she move into the residence until things cool down. She only lives five houses down the block, but needs to keep a watchful eye on Emily. She will have her conversation with him on Friday when he comes back home. She would not dare interrupt him at work; he doesn't need to be bothered by something as trivial as Emily thinking she can get out of this marriage. There is no way Kyndall will allow something so preposterous. She takes the manila envelope with her downstairs to make herself a sandwich and wait on Emily; she will need her strength to fight this fight.

Chapter 6

mily drops the children off at school and head back home. When she pulls up in front of the house, she sees Kyndall's black Mercedes. Emily grips the steering wheel and holds her head down while saying to herself, "Not today." Emily doesn't have the strength for her combative mother-in-law. She needs something to help ease the tension. She searches her purse for her anxiety medication and takes the pill with a sip of water. As the pill slowly digests, she crawls out of the car with calculated methodical moves and makes it to the front door. The keys are in her right hand as she concentrates on inserting the key in the lock. Her hand trembles, not from the medication, but from the thought of having to interact with Kyndall. She finally aligns the key and turns it to the right; but finds she needs the full strength of her body to turn the knob and open the door. She steps inside the foyer and takes a deep breath. She can never let Kyndall know how much she unnerves her, and put on her best performance. It's show time!

Emily uses her best cheery voice. "Hello, Kyndall?"

"I'm in the kitchen!"

Emily walks into the kitchen and immediately notices the manila envelope on the granite counter top next to the fruit bowl. She knows that her mother-in-law purposefully placed the envelope so she could see it when she entered the kitchen. Kyndall comes from behind the counter and greets Emily with a hug and kiss on the cheek.

"How are you, Emily?"

"I am doing well, what about you?" Emily acts cool as though the manila envelope didn't mean anything.

Emily thinks back to the events of the morning and swears that she put the envelope back in the drawer. Did Kyndall rummage through her closet and find the divorce papers?

Kyndall sinks her teeth into a turkey and cheese sandwich; to Emily, her bites seem small and calculated. "I think she wants to throw me off my game by paying so much attention to those damn chips and sandwich." Emily shifts her weight from her right foot to her left as Kyndall moves from the sandwich, to the chips, and takes a big gulp of her Diet Coke.

Immediately, Kyndall notices and a light twinkle behind her eyes. Oh, how she loves to make Emily feel uncomfortable by creating tension in the air. She does not speak, simply lets her wonder how much she knows about her plans to leave Brendon.

After Kyndall moves through her lunch in the precise three steps, she takes her last sip of the diet drink and says, "So, Emily, what have you been up to lately?"

Emily pauses before replying. If she takes the bait, Kyndall has her cornered. Should she confess and tell Kyndall about wanting a divorce? There is no time to vet each choice thoroughly, so Emily drops the glass she is holding to buy some time to sort out her spinning thoughts. Before Kyndall can say anything, Emily rushes to the laundry room to get the broom and dust pan to clean up the broken glass and pools of water. Emily slowly sweeps the shards into the trash can and mops up the expanding pools. She then moves to the kitchen sink and makes a big deal of washing her hands by rubbing them excessively under the lukewarm water. Kyndall steals side glances at her when she finally dries her hands. Emily has built up the courage to tell Kyndall to go to hell, but instead she reaches for the envelope and turns to walk out of the kitchen. Kyndall is stunned by Emily's actions. "Where are you going? We need to talk."

Emily says, "I'm going upstairs to start my work day."

"I know you want to divorce Brendon," Kyndall yells, following Emily from the kitchen to the living room.

As Emily advances up the stairs with each step, she gains more control. "The intimate details of my marriage are off limits to you and all other outsiders. If we need you to intervene, Brendon and I will include you in the conversation. I refuse to have a conversation with you about the stability of my marriage; it's not fair to Brendon and I want to give him the courtesy of a face-to-face conversation. You will not talk to him about this. Do you understand?"

Kyndall raises her voice from the stairs below and makes a bold statement. "If you want to blame someone for your miserable life, then you need to start with your mother."

She grabs her purse and keys and heads toward the door.

Emily races back down the stairs and shouts, "What did you say about my mother?"

Kyndall playfully tosses her keys in the air and catches them several times before turning around to face Emily, slowly. "Emily, you walk around here with your head down feeling sorry for yourself, but you need to look around and appreciate what the Lord has given you. You have two beautiful children and a house that has increased in value and is now worth in the ballpark of one million dollars, yet you walk around telling yourself how miserable you are. You knew what you were getting into when you married Brendon and my aspirations for my family. You don't cry when you take vacation in the Hamptons in the family house during the Fourth of July or even when you have dinner with Robin Givens at the second family house at Hilton Head Island."

Emily screams, "That's not fair! You ruined the life that I was supposed to have."

Emily is holding back the tears; she refuses to let Kyndall see her cry. She takes two short breaths while blowing air out of her mouth to regain control of her emotions.

"My dear Emily, are you talking about the little lesbian relationship you wanted with what's-her-name?" Kyndall pauses to think back to recall the name. "Oh yeah... *Julia*. I saved you from yourself. You were confused then and you are confused now to think that you will have a better life without me and Brendon. So, what do you think? Do you think you are going to pick back up where you and Julia left off and play house? From what I remember, she married that pervert professor at Temple, Mr. Banks, yeah, the one who used to prey on the innocence of his graduate students. You of all people should remember what a menace he was."

Emily ignores the comment. This conversation isn't going anywhere, and she knows that Kyndall is right about so many things. She is a mess because she has lost herself in taking care of everyone else's needs. If she leaves Brendon, where will she go? She has nothing. She has no money other than what is in a secret account she shares with her mother, but needs to hang on to as much of that as she can for emergencies. Emily needs a plan and needs to be self-sufficient. *Am I delusional to think that Julia would want me after all these years?* Emily sits on the stairs and starts to cry; it is no longer important for Kyndall not to see.

"You win, Kyndall! You win!"

"Emily, do you think this is a game? You, Brendon, and the twins are my life, and that will never change. This family will stay together because of our strong family values. The American people will understand who we are and what we stand for. Nothing will come between the unity we share as a family. Not a bi-curious woman who kissed a girl once in a bar. Yes, Emily, I know what happened; there isn't much I don't know at Temple. I am on the Board of Trustees and keep my ear to the streets; there are people who tell me things in exchange for certain favors. They scratch my back and I scratch theirs. Do you really think that the American people want to see you, Brendon, Madison, Connor, and Julia living in the White House?"

Kyndall laughs as she visualizes the five of them in the White House. "In between press interviews Julia is slipping her hand up your skirt and kissing you in the halls of the White House? That image doesn't scream family values."

"Stop it! I get it! I am trapped and you did this to me."

"No, Emily, your mother did this to you."

"You keep bringing my mother's name up. What happened between you and my mother?"

Kyndall's response is flip and dismissive. "I don't get involved in family secrets, just the ones that impact me. Look, Emily, it's obvious that you need some time away. Why don't you go to one of the vacation homes and take some time for yourself? Get yourself together, emotionally. I can't have you falling apart in front of the television cameras."

Emily murmurs, "I don't want to go to the Hamptons or even to Hilton Head Island."

Kyndall chuckles. "Right, poor Emily doesn't want this privileged life. Okay, have it your way." She reaches in her purse and pulls out a business card and places it on the end table near the door. Kyndall moves her hand to her face and smooths her right eyebrow while closing her right eye to give the impression she is annoyed. "Emily, it is obvious you are troubled and need sometime away. I own a home in North Carolina and think that you need some time to get yourself together for Brendon's run for the White House. My friends Emma and Harold live across the street from the house and will take care of you once you arrive. Harold's name and phone number are on the card. Please be discreet in everything that you do; remember, you will one day be the first lady and don't need bad publicity." Kyndall turns and head for the door to once again try to leave.

Without turning around, she says, "You can thank me later for giving you this chance to live your life. Ta ta." And just like that, the Wicked Witch of Society Hill disappears.

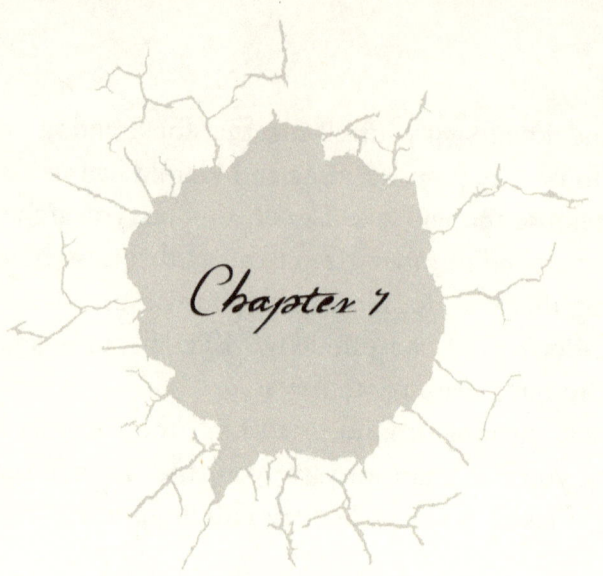

Chapter 7

Emily wipes the tears on the back of her hand and races upstairs to find her cell phone in her purse. She quickly locates her mother's contact information and hits voice call.

Doris answers the phone on the second ring. "Hello?"

"Mother, what have you done?"

Emily doesn't have to say another word; Doris knew that one day she would have to explain her decision, but didn't think it would be now. Perhaps on her death bed, but not now. Doris takes a deep breath; she knows what she is about to tell her dear daughter will hurt her to the core. She starts to speak, but nothing comes out, so quietly she whimpers. Eventually, the whimpers turn into uncontrollable sobs.

Emily gets impatient and through clenched teeth says once again, "Mother. What. Have. You. Done?"

Doris reaches for a tissue and dries her eyes and then blows her nose, each step giving her more time to get up the courage to expose the shameful act she committed years ago.

In a low whisper, Doris starts to speak. "Sweetheart, it was such a long time ago. I didn't know what else to do when your father lost his job. We were already living from paycheck to pay-check; my disability check was barely taking care of the bills and the house payment got behind. You were close to graduation; I needed to do what I could to help with your school fees. I knew we couldn't live in the house much longer without paying the mortgage. Each day, I felt my chest tighten as I pulled the door to the mailbox down. Each piece of mail I would go through quickly, looking for any correspondence from the bank. The day we received the foreclosure notification, I was sitting on the front porch worried about how we were going to make it without a roof over our heads. We had thirty days to vacate the property. It didn't matter to me if they gave us six months to leave. We just didn't have any place to go and no family to depend on."

Doris remembers pulling the wad of tissues out of her pant pocket and dabbing the corners of her eyes. The tears start to flow at this point.

* * *

A fancy Mercedes had pulled into the driveway and a beautiful lady who stood five-foot-nine, with a smile that could charm a con man to buy his own elixir, sashayed up the walkway and approached her on the porch. Doris had tried to get herself together by drying her eyes and blowing her nose before the mystery lady reached the porch. Too late. Kyndall Graham introduced herself with an extended hand. Doris wiped her right hand on her shirt and extended it to shake with this stranger.

"It is nice to meet you, Mrs. Graham. My name is Doris Massey."

Kyndall attempted to put Doris at ease. "Please, call me Kyndall."

"Please have a seat. Would you care for some ice tea?"

"No, thank you," said Kyndall before settling down beside Doris on the swing.

Kyndall had seen that Doris was upset. "Are you okay?" She glanced over at the letter Doris had in her hand and noted the bold "foreclosure notification" in large red letters. Doris tried to quickly place the letter back in the envelope to shield it from Kyndall. The last thing she needed was someone feeling sorry for her and her family, especially this high society city woman.

The foreclosure notification had given Kyndall another angle to work. She cleared her throat. "I am the mother of Emily's boyfriend, Brendon Graham. My husband is Wellington Graham, attorney general for the State of Pennsylvania. I think that I can speak for both my husband and myself when I say we have high aspirations for our son and are grooming him to be the senator for Pennsylvania and then on to the White House as President. I have been there for both men in my life and have supported them in reaching all our aspirations. I come from humble beginnings, but always knew that with hard work and dedication I would be able to make my dreams come true. And I want the same for Brendon. There is a path that great leaders take early in their lives which defines what and who they will become later in life. It starts with a college education, community service, aspiration, family values, and finding the right mate. There needs to be someone by your side who will stand by you no matter what. I see Emily as that person for Brendon. She has strong family values and can help him stay on track. I will not always be there for him, and I need to know that once I am dead and gone he has someone who will do anything to help him succeed. She's loyal, and that's what I am looking for."

Silently, Doris stared at Kyndall, who took it as a deafening sign of disapproval. She decided to change her tactic. "How much do you need to save the house?"

Doris wrinkled her brow and tightened her grip on the

envelope. Kyndall reached over to touch Doris's hand, but she quickly stood up to avoid her touch.

"Are you blackmailing me to encourage my daughter to marry your boy? Emily hasn't told me everything, but I can draw my own conclusions as to what type of person he is. If he wasn't messed up in the head, you wouldn't need to offer me money to persuade my daughter to marry Brendon. You should be ashamed of yourself by even coming here to ask me to do this," Doris huffed in a whisper.

Kyndall reached in her purse and pulled out her checkbook. She wrote Doris a personal check for $50,000 and placed it on the chair where Doris was sitting, along with her personal business card.

"You have two choices: cash the check and keep the house; don't cash the check and live on the street. This is a win-win for everybody when you come to your senses and cash the check. I am trying to do what any good mother would do. I want my son to have the best life he possibly can, and in return, if Emily marries Brendon, she will have a privileged life. Isn't that what all mothers want, to know their children will be taken care of? I will make sure you and Emily have the life you dreamed. Remember, cashing the check means you will uphold your end of the deal."

Kyndall stood and smoothed the wrinkles in her white linen pants. They were her favorite as they had the drawstring waist, which made her figure more of an hourglass. She reached for her purse and found her sunglasses, which she slipped down over her face. She extended her hand to Doris. "It was a pleasure meeting you."

It had taken every ounce of courage for Doris to find her manners. Reluctantly, she extended her hand to shake the hand of the woman she wished she never met. Kyndall walked off the porch and fished for her keys; she unlocked the car and elegantly slid into the driver side. One turn of the switch ignited the engine.

She pushed her sunglasses to the bridge of her nose and peered over the top to take a second glance at Doris. Doris spotted her and quickly moved toward the front door, leaving the check where Kyndall left it on the porch. Kyndall wasn't sure how long it would take Doris to cash the check but knew she was a woman after her own heart; she would never let her family fall apart.

Chapter 8

It took Doris fifteen days to cash the check. Sadly, she remembered the exact day. She had received a call from Emily saying that she was coming home for spring break to spend time with her mother and to catch up on sleep, and of course she needed to wash her clothes. Doris had laughed—going off to college was supposed to be the first step in a young person's independence. She had found it amusing that Emily was so proud to let her know that, but couldn't seem to wash her clothes without her mother's help.

Doris had shaken her head, but smiled. "I would love to see you."

There was pain behind her eyes as she spoke. The dreaded thought had entered Doris's head…the week of spring break was after they needed to be out of the house, and they wouldn't have any place to go. Emily would no longer have a room and her own bed to sleep in. Emily hadn't noticed the darkness in her voice because she was talking nonstop about school, Brendon, and her friend Julia. Doris had been glad that the conversation between

the two of them was over the phone because Emily could not notice her facial expression. Fortunately, Emily also hadn't noticed
how Doris had stayed mostly quiet, listening to Emily chatter on.
Emily had asked Doris a question that brought her back to reality,
and she needed to focus to answer.

"Can Julia stay a few days during spring break?"

"Oh, of course, Emily, any of your friends can stay. I enjoy
having the company."

After, Emily had ended the call by saying that she loved her
mother and couldn't wait to see her. Doris walked over to her jew-
elry box and pulled out her mortgage coupon book, along with
the check Kyndall had written. She searched for a pen and signed
the back of the check before putting it in her purse, along with
the mortgage coupon book. Doris moved quickly from the back
of the house where her bedroom was to the front door. She removed her house keys from the decorative key holder that stored
her purse and keys. After all, she was a stickler for order and everything had to have a place. Doris had unlocked the front door
and closed it behind her as she walked down the stairs and turned
right toward the bank. Her mind made up, she walked with pur-
pose. Nothing would stop her from saving her house and her
family.

* * *

Emily can't believe what she is hearing. *How could she have tak-
en money from Kyndall?* Even though Emily says that she doesn't
understand, she does. Keeping the family intact has always been
important to her mother.

Emily starts to rub her temples with her fingers. *Can this day
get any worse?*" she thinks. It can. In rapid succession, Emily receives ten text messages in her inbox. Emily put the phone on
speaker to continue to listen to her mother apologize for taking
the bribe from Kyndall while opening each text message, one at a
time. She gasps, and places her hand over her mouth in awe. Each

photo is of Brendon and an unidentified female doing drugs, lounging nude, or drinking. There is drug paraphernalia in many of the photos, and one taken on the balcony with the city skyline in the background. Emily doesn't know if these photos are recent or old. All Emily knows is Brendon isn't home and she doesn't know what to do. Emily stands and paces back and forth in the bedroom, thinking. She doesn't have anyone else to talk to about this, and decides she should call Kyndall. Maybe she is still outside. Emily picks the phone up off the bed and races down the stairs. She stares out the front window to find both Pearl and Kyndall talking in front of the house. "Mother, may I call you back?"

"I know that you are upset and don't want to talk to me, but I love you so much. I wanted you to have a better life." Doris continues to talk and Emily senses that if she doesn't tell her mother she is forgiven she will never be able to get her off the phone.

"I forgive you, Mother."

Those words soothe Doris's ears; she can't bear to live with her daughter upset at her. Doris smiles, knowing that Emily, her only daughter, can find it in her heart to forgive her. Doris knows that taking the money from Kyndall was the right decision at the time, but also that she hurt Emily by making the deal. She need to make things right between them, even though Emily has said that all is forgiven.

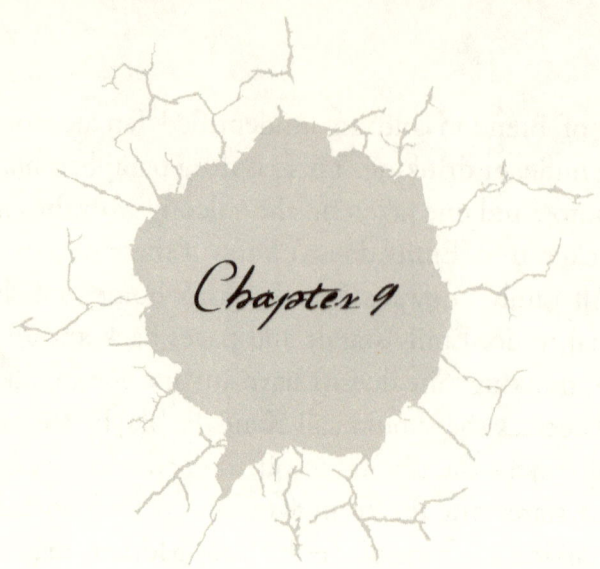

oris chews on her bottom left lip as she replays the conversation with Emily in her head. Emily has had the privileged life that Kyndall promised, but the hell she has gone through with both Brendon and Kyndall has been too much for Doris to hear about. Doris believes that Emily can find love again and be happy, even if she doesn't have the world at her feet. Just some peace is all Doris wants for Emily, love and peace.

Doris pulls out her iPad and Google's the name Julia Sutton Banks. It takes her fifteen minutes and a search through Facebook, LinkedIn, and YouTube to find the correct person. She smiles as she watches the videos that display Julia's life from the time that she married David Banks to her accolades within the field of engineering. Doris can understand why Emily was so smitten with Julia. She's smart, ambitious, and beautiful—what a combination. Doris combs through all the information that she finds on Julia, and after two hours of catching up on Julia's life, she sends her a message on Facebook, leaving her contact information. Just as Doris logs off the iPad, she receives a call from an unidentified caller. Thank goodness for social media.

"Doris, this is Julia. How are you?"

"It is so great to hear from you! I am doing well."

"I'm surprised you reached out to me. I never thought you cared for me that much."

"Julia, that's the reason I am reaching out to you. I wanted to tell you I am ashamed for what I did when you visited my house on spring break. I wasn't the best hostess, nor did I show you the type of hospitality that I would expect guests to show me in their home. I reached out to you because I want to apologize for my actions years ago. I feel as though I was the reason that you and Emily never moved forward with your relationship. A mother knows deep in her heart when her child is in love. I saw it in your eyes how you felt for Emily. For my part in breaking the two of you up, I apologize."

Julia gasps. An apology from Doris is the last thing she expects. A million memories come flooding back as Julia starts to cry.

"Why now? Why are you reaching out to me now? Emily and I have both moved on with our lives, and from what I hear, she is living a wonderful life with the handsome senator from the State of Pennsylvania and two beautiful children. Why now, Doris?"

"That's a fair question. Emily is hurting right now, and she needs some peace and a sense of calm in her life. I know she had that when the two of you were together. You would have had a great life together, but I interfered when I shouldn't have."

"You have mentioned several times that you were the reason Emily and I aren't together. I don't see the connection."

Doris gives Julia the *Reader's Digest* version of the story. "I pushed Brendon and Emily together and didn't take into consideration how they felt for each other. I didn't let Emily decide who she wanted to be with. For my part, again, I am sorry I hurt the two of you."

"Thank you, Doris. You don't know how much it means to hear you apologize. I thought I had done something to offend Emily and that was why she moved on without me. How is Emily by the way?"

"When you are looking at her life on television and on paper it is wonderful, but if you are with her for any length of time, you know she isn't happy."

"Do you mind giving Emily my phone number?"

"I would be happy to give her the phone number, but I think that she would love to hear from you. Please take her number."

The two of them exchange pleasantries for the next twenty minutes and hang up with the promises to keep in touch. Doris smiles as she realizes how deeply she means it when she says she hopes to see Julia soon.

Chapter 10

Julia ends the call with Doris and immediately lifts herself from the chaise in the bedroom she shares with Dave. She glides to the window and stares at the trees and children playing in the street. Stanley, the son she and Dave adopted is standing outside in the yard, watching the younger children play dodge ball. Stanley had been moved through the foster care system due to the unexpected death of his mother, Deidre. When Deidre died of a heart attack and all the children had to be moved, Stanley had been scheduled to be moved to the home of Pearl Johnson, but she was no longer accepting children. Julia and Dave had been working with social services to adopt a baby, but changed their minds instantly when they were introduced to Stanley.

Stanley seemed shy when he interacted with Julia and Dave; he stayed quiet and alert during their meetings, drawing pictures of his idea of a happy family. There was one picture that he drew of Julia, Dave, and himself holding hands while looking at their dream home from the outside. Julia discussed with Stanley how she wanted them to be a family, with a soft squeeze of the hand.

She thought Stanley wanted the security of a family. Julia did everything in her power to compensate him for being in the foster care system, which contributed to his poor human interactions.

Stanley was shy at first, but he warmed up to both Dave and Julia after several months. There was only one topic he would not discuss: living in the foster care system. Stanley often refused to have the conversation or just walked out the room. Dave and Julia knew that Stanley had a secret, but weren't quite sure what it was. What they did know was it began to consume him.

He often spent hours alone and his style became more Gothic. He looked morbid with his pale skin, black hair, black lips, and all-black clothing, down to the boots and socks. The black eyeliner and nail polish scared Julia as he got older. The more he embraced this style, the more secluded he became.

His personality is becoming as dark as his clothing, Julia thinks as she stares out the window. Worry furrows her brow. She is startled back to reality by the clatter of a rock against glass and sees the smug smile playing at the corners of Stanley's lips. "Why does he have to be an ass," she grumbles and backs away from the window. She paces back and forth. Her thoughts turn from her son and his seemingly painful past to her own.

There are so many reasons why she shouldn't call Emily. So much time has passed and she isn't sure if she should dredge up old feelings. For what? They both have moved on with fulfilled lives. Julia loves her Dave, but Doris paints a different picture of Emily and Brendon. It sounds like the two of them are together out of obligation more than anything. Is it true? Can Doris be trusted? Julia tells herself that there are two sides of the story and Doris is giving her story, the side of an outsider. Julia is more convinced now than ever that she should call Emily; they should at least connect by phone. "There is no time like the present," Julia says out loud to no one. She picks up her cell phone again and dials Emily's number, which goes straight to voice mail. "Emily, hi;

this is Julia. I know it's been a long time since the two of us have spoken. How are you? Your mom found me through Facebook and she and I connected this afternoon; she gave me your phone number. I hope that's okay with you. I know I am rambling; I guess I am a bit nervous. Give me a call if you want to talk."

Dave watches Julia intensely while she cradles the phone like a school girl. He hears the entire conversation. Julia thinks she is the only person who loved Emily, but he, too, had feelings for her. He didn't love her, but lusted after her as he did all his conquests.

Dave has always been aware of his weakness for young coeds with perky breasts and shapely hips. Prior to marrying Julia, Dave had been married to Debra, his first wife, for ten years. Over the course of their marriage, Dave became more indifferent toward his relationship with Debra and reckless with his encounters. Debra filed for divorce because she was tired of Dave's "indiscretions." He had been unfaithful for years, but when she caught him in their bed having sex with Caitlyn, his graduate assistant, that was the last straw.

Debra knew that Dave was up to no good on that day. He had gotten up early and fixed Debra breakfast, and asked her several times about her schedule for the day. At first, Debra said that she didn't have any plans, but when she saw the desperate look in his eyes, she told him she had an appointment and then lunch with Tonya. If Dave had been attentive to Debra, he would have known she was lying. Tonya and Debra had had a falling out six months earlier when Tonya told Debra to leave Dave. Her heart sank when Dave didn't question the story other than to ask what time she was leaving. But she said nothing. Instead, she dressed, kissed her husband on the cheek, and left the house through the garage. She backed their Toyota Prius down the driveway, disappearing into the distance.

After Debra left, Dave called Caitlyn and gave her the address of his home. They chatted for a while, with Caitlyn saying the "L" word. Dave heard the comment, but hung up so he didn't have to go into an explanation of why he didn't say he loved her back. Dave didn't do the touchy-feely expressions with his graduate students. He stuck to his belief that they agreed that it was "about fun" when they started messing around. Fun became problematic when the young students began to "catch feelings." Once they began to want more, it was time to move on to the next graduate assistant. This was a perk in the university's system. He could have a different girl every semester if he wanted.

Caitlyn took a taxi over to meet Dave at his home.

She arrived wearing a black trench coat with the lace bra and panties he had purchased the day before at Victoria's Secret. The heels were an added touch to her classy, but slutty look. Either way Dave was turned on. It made him sad to think about parting ways. They had sex on the sofa and moved before tumbling up the stairs and into bed, far too distracted to hear the door open and close; just as Luther Vandross crooned, "Always and Forever," an "Oh hell no!" startled them into stunned silence. Dave rolled off Caitlyn to see Debra standing there.

Caitlyn ran into the bathroom, crying rather loudly. Dave rolled his eyes. *What did she expect having sex in a married man's home? We were bound to get caught, eventually.* He couldn't help but smirk at the thought.

"Caitlyn, stop crying, it's going to be okay."

Dave slowly started to dress. The sound of Debra screaming and the smash of her fists against his chest seemed overboard. Dave grabbed her by the wrists to prevent her from striking again.

"You act like you don't know why I cheat. You stopped having sex with me two years ago. We went from making love four days a week to one day and then you would have one excuse after another why you didn't want to be with me, your husband. I offered to go to counseling, but you refused. Instead, you told me that your girlfriends said that there was more to a relationship than sex and we should try to connect on 'another level.' Did you ever once think that I might have needed sex to connect?"

In the wake of Debra's silence, Dave's thoughts turned not to the slender woman hugging the toilet from behind the locked bathroom door, but to another of his desired conquests—the promising undergraduate in his Psych 100 class. Dave had tried "mental stimulation" activities for two days and just gave up. Weak and longing for the touch of a woman, he felt himself grow rigid as Emily strolled into his classroom. The cotton of his pants felt constricting when he called her name during roll call. Emily was different than the other college students. She was studious and came to class prepared to ask thought-provoking questions. When Dave moved from right to left, lecturing about Skinner's theory, Emily hung onto his every word. She typed a little, raised her hand, and asked another series of questions. Dave felt her eyes; they were locked on him as he educated her on the study of psychology. His head spun as he thought about feeding her the knowledge that she obviously craved. He knew she wanted him.

Ironically, Emily had been a source of contention, not between Debra and himself, but between himself and Caitlyn. A week earlier, she had been the subject of a fight.

"Oh my god, you asked me to find out where she lived. You told me you were concerned that she missed class!"

"Don't be a jealous bitch, it's not becoming of you. I was concerned that my star pupil was absent."

In truth, the one and only day she missed class had provided the perfect excuse to show "concern" for his "little angel" and visit her dorm room. He had taken a liking to Emily, not only because she was sexy, but because she exuded innocence.

"You don't check on all your absent students—why her?"

Dave had to bite back his reply. He was not ready to admit that he was obsessed with Emily. He watched her when she walked from her last class to the dining hall, every Wednesday. His office in the Liberal Arts building provided the perfect view. He would time it just right, and made sure Sheryl, the academic assistant, didn't schedule any advising appointments during the fifteen minutes before and after Emily's weekly stroll. Dave locked his door, positioned his chair in front of the window, and unzipped his pants, breathing a sigh of relief as tension eased. His hand would find the bulge and massage it. The faster she walked, the faster he rubbed, until he released, uttering her name in sheer ecstasy. By the time she closed the dining hall doors, he was finished.

"You are sick," Caitlyn spat. "Tammy and Rebekah warned me about you. I should have listened."

"Caitlyn, no one likes a gossip. Keep your fucking mouth shut."

Her jealousy was distracting him from his reverie. He had strolled over to Emily's dorm to find the door ajar. He peeped inside to find Emily's towel slip from around her waist to the floor. She reached for the lotion and started to lather her body. Dave could no longer control his urges. Without thinking, he found himself inside the room and managed to shut the door behind him. As Emily bent to slather lotion on her sexy legs, he pulled his penis out of his pants and pounced on her from behind. *She doesn't need to turn around*, he told himself. *She can handle me and all I have to offer.*

Dave knew that Emily was planning to cut his class because of the conversation she had with Brendon outside of his class the week before. He had lingered at the front of the room, slowly erasing the board. Emily and Brendon had been having trouble finding time to see each other, and the only option was for her to miss Dave's class. *I just need to find out where she lives*, he thought. Dave gathered his lecture notes and turned out the lights. He had a plan for the next week…he just needed Caitlyn to cover for him for the first fifteen minutes of class.

When Emily climaxed, she screamed Brendon's name, but

Dave imagined that it was his. Dave thrust his body into hers as if desperate to suck every drop of her sweetness. Emily and he climaxed together. As she collapsed on the floor, he zipped his pants and gently closed the door behind him.

"You son of a bitch, how can you be so cold and callous? You only care about yourself."

Caitlyn's whining brought him back to reality.

"Maybe so, but I love what I see in the mirror."

Chapter ii

"*I* thought you loved me," Caitlyn sniveled when she opened the bathroom door, ignoring the enraged woman who was still trying to claw at her lover's chest.

"Love you? Don't act like a delusional little girl."

Caitlyn flung a towel around her naked body. "I am leaving."

"I think that's best."

"I never want to see you again."

"Well, that will be hard since you work for me," Dave sneered.

Caitlyn brushed past both Dave and Debra in her rush for the bedroom door. She dressed as she hobbled down the stairs, leaving Debra and Dave to fend for themselves. "I hope she kills him," she muttered as she tightened the trench coat around her waist and started down the street, heels in hand.

As the disillusioned girl with the tear-stained face began her walk of shame, Debra reached under the bed and pulled out a suitcase so she could haphazardly pack Dave's clothes. She pulled a second suitcase out from behind the bed skirt for his toiletries.

With steel in her face, she picked up the oversized bags and handed them to Dave.

"Please leave and don't come back."

"Are you sure this is what you want? Once I leave I won't come back."

"I would appreciate that. Leave your key on the hallway table."

Without a word, Dave did just that.

Chapter 12

*U*naware that Dave is likewise reminiscing about Emily's college days, Julia remembers her own with Emily. Pain stabs her in the chest as the memory of her graduation night plays on the movie screen behind her eyelids.

* * *

Julia had finally built up the nerve to tell Emily how she truly felt for her when Samantha, her girlfriend at the time, arrived. Julia knew that she had been holding Samantha at bay once she had come to grips with her true feelings for Emily. She wasn't sure how Emily would take it if she confessed her feelings.

Emily had lived a sheltered life and wasn't accustomed to self-expression. She had lived a life believing that the body one was born into, female or male, dictated one's lifestyle. If a person thought they wanted to date the same sex, they were confused and needed to ask the Lord for forgiveness as these weren't pure thoughts. At least twice a year, Emily's grandfather, who was a pastor, preached a sermon condemning those who were living an alternative lifestyle and their souls burning in hell for the shame they brought to the church. Gays and lesbians were not allowed to work in his church, and could only be in attendance if they were repenting for their sins. Emily, the pleasing daughter and granddaughter, sat still, listening intensely to her grandfather's sermon, and vowed never to disobey God; hell, was such a bad place for people who were evil. These thoughts rested in the back of Emily's mind throughout her young adult life.

Julia was not so repressed. It nearly killed her, but she kept quiet about the way she felt, afraid of coming on too strong, lest she push Emily away. Emily was not ready to accept that they were connecting in ways that were deeper than a sexual relationship. Emily completed her sentences, and she was in her head, every day. It was Emily who consumed Julia's thoughts as Samantha kissed her. Julia pulled herself away to discover that Emily was running out to the bar. She turned to follow, but the pain ripping through her chest as she watched Emily fall into Brendon's arms and kiss him stopped her in her tracks. Emily's absence sucked the heat from the room and blurred Julia's vision. Through her haze, she barely acknowledged the good wishes and "congratulations on the big day." All she could think about was a life without Emily.

"Samantha, we need to talk."

They headed outside where the sky was clear. Initiating the conversation with Samantha was uncomfortable and painful for Julia because they had been together ever since they were sixteen years old, kissing in the bathroom at school during lunch. They had proclaimed their love for each other and didn't care who knew how they felt. Both had applied to Temple and received acceptance letters. They had lived together for the first year; however, Samantha had to move back home after their freshman year to care for her ill mother. Julia had needed to find a roommate for the sophomore school year. That was when she met Emily. Julia had been serving as a university ambassador, and noticed Emily from afar, once she entered the auditorium. She was awkward, clumsy, and needed refinement. Julia was willing to take on a special project to help Emily find her inner beauty.

As Julia thought about how Emily and she met, she noticed Samantha nervously biting her lower lip; she knew that the relationship had been over for months, but didn't have the willpower to have the conversation. Graduation night was the last straw. She had to get Samantha to know that for the last three years, she had secretly loved Emily. There were many nights Julia had watched Emily sleep. She looked so peaceful and innocent. She had wanted to protect her from any and everyone who wanted to hurt her, intentionally or unintentionally. She had kept a watchful eye on Brendon, the privileged freshman who had a crush on Emily. She was not sure what Emily saw in that guy, but knew that he was her competition in winning her over and securing a future together.

Although Julia felt torn up about hurting Samantha, she could not wait to tell Emily the news. She flew toward the dorm they shared, eager to start their life together. Julia unlocked the door, hoping to see Emily, who left the bar hours prior. She sat on the bed, taking her shoes off and throwing them in the corner. She curled up in a fetal position and cried herself to sleep.

Chapter 13

Emily hadn't returned by the next morning. When Julia turned over and saw the pristine sheets, she softly wept. She lay there for a few more hours, until she could no longer deny that Emily would not return. Only then did she begin to clear out her side of the room. As she loaded her car, she bumped into Professor Banks, her psychology instructor. He could see that Julia wasn't her usual self and asked what was wrong.

She cried an ocean of tears before the story came spilling out of her mouth. "I broke up with Samantha to be with Emily, but Emily left the bar last night with Brendon and I haven't heard from her since."

Professor Dave Banks helped her pack her car and they walked to his office. Dave opened the door and asked Julia to sit on the sofa.

"Professor, I really appreciate your taking the time to speak with me but I am okay."

"Obviously, you're not; you are shaking."

"I am torn up inside. I thought she loved me; we shared a kiss that made my heart flutter. I thought she loved me too…that was why I initiated the kiss." Julia was aware how Emily stared at her. Her pupils enlarged at the sight of her. "Did I misread Emily?"

Dave sat there in disbelief that he had to contend with Julia, a woman, for Emily's love. His grip on his pen was so tight, his hand started to bleed from the clip digging into his index finger. The only response Dave had for Julia was selfish. "What if she doesn't feel the same way about you? Are you prepared to move forward?"

"No, I want to live my life with her. I left her a letter in the dorm expressing my undying love for her."

"I see. Do you think that leaving her the letter was a good idea?"

"I don't know what else to do! She did see me and Samantha kiss, but she doesn't know I broke up with Samantha. Dr. Banks, it's getting late. I need to head home, or my mother will start to worry."

"Are you going to be okay to drive?"

"Yes, I will be fine. I just need to get myself together. Is there a ladies' room?"

"Of course, down the hall on the right."

"Thank you, Dr. Banks, for all of your help."

"You are so welcome. You have my card; call me if you ever want to talk." "Yes, of course, being able to talk through my feelings is helpful."

Julia left Dr. Banks' office and walked down the narrow hallway toward the ladies' room. Dr. Banks cracked his office door, saw Julia close the door to the ladies' room behind her, and darted down the hallway to the back stairs. Perspiration formed on his upper lip and forehead as he walked briskly toward Julia's dorm to retrieve the letter Julia left for Emily.

"There is no way in hell I will surrender to Emily. What a waste, two women who love each other in *that* way."

He entered the dorm through a side door and took the stairs to the second floor. Dr. Banks placed his credit card between the door and lock; it took him very little effort to break the flimsy lock. He gently and quietly closed the door behind him, giving the room a 360-degree scan. The room looked different than what he remembered, in part because Julia had moved out of the dorm, but largely because the last time he had been there, he hadn't focused on learning anything about its design. He had been focused on fulfilling his fantasy of Emily, which he did, and ever since, he couldn't forget about her and the sweet lovemaking that happened between the two of them. After sex with Emily, nothing Caitlyn or his wife could do for him matched the softness of her skin and how she pleasured him. Dr. Banks ran his hand across Emily's bed, remembering her soft lips and curvy hips. He had to force himself to look around for the object that had occasioned the break-in: the letter. He found it on Emily's dresser. Dave picked the dreaded document up and tore it into tiny pieces, which he tossed into the toilet, flushing the evidence of Julia's love for Emily away. The pieces floated from side to side in the basin until the suction emptied the bowl clean. Dave smiled at the thought that there was nothing left of the memories of Julia and Emily.

Chapter 14

*J*ulia walked across campus to her dorm to pick up her last piece of luggage and to check if Emily had made it back. She unlocked the door and grabbed the handle of her suitcase, sitting in the middle of the floor. Julia sighed and held back the tears of disappointment, burning each time she blinked. Emily brought her joy and pushed her to be the best person that she could be; she was the reason Julia had just been hired at Westinghouse Electric as a project manager.

As Julia exited the room she turned, glanced around one last time, and remembered the excitement she felt loving Emily. Chills moved from her legs to her arms. She shook as she closed the door and walked toward her new future, leaving the memories of Emily behind.

Chapter 15

*J*ulia had a few weeks before starting a new job at Westinghouse Electric in Eastover, South Carolina. She passed the time with her parents, who reluctantly helped her prepare for the move. Her mother took her shopping for a professional wardrobe. Julia obediently went through the motions of trying on skirts and suits, pretending to be interested in moving on. Julia's thoughts replayed leaving the note for Emily to call her when she came back to the room. *Why wouldn't she call me? Did she feel the same way that I felt for her? I can't bear the thought of not being with her.* When Julia arrived at the house, she took the bags up to her room and set them down in the closet. She didn't have the heart to put away her new clothes. New clothes meant new beginnings, and she just wasn't ready to live a life without her love. Instead, she picked up her cell phone to call Emily for the tenth time that day, but couldn't bring herself to punch the familiar numbers. When she set the phone beside her, she noticed she had two missed calls from Dr. Banks. She picked up the phone, hoping that listening to the messages would give her the courage to follow through with the call to Emily.

Julia put the phone on speaker and played the messages.

"Hi Julia, this is Mr. Banks. I wanted to know if you were okay. I haven't heard from you. Please give me a call."

The second message was a repeat of the first. She deleted both messages and wondered how Mr. Banks got her cell phone number. It was very kind of him to take the time to listen to her the other day, so she decided to return his call.

"Hello, Mr. Banks, this is Julia. How are you?"

"Julia, it is so good to hear from you. I know you were distraught when we spoke the other day and I wanted to check on you. Are you still sorting through your feelings for Emily?"

"I mean…I love her but I don't know why she didn't call me after I left her the note professing my love for her, and she hasn't reached out to me. I guess I am more disappointed in myself for thinking the bond we had was mutual."

The mischievous smile on Dave's face made it difficult for him to gather his thoughts to respond to Julia's comments. The silence was awkward.

"Hello, Mr. Banks, are you still there?"

"Oh yes, Julia, I was just thinking that we should start your sessions soon. When do you leave for your new job?"

"The job doesn't start for another two weeks, but I need to leave Philadelphia to put the memories of Emily behind."

"Okay, can you meet me in my office tomorrow at noon? Perhaps we can talk through your feelings over lunch in my office." Dave moved his hand over the growing bulge in his pants as he thought about Emily too.

"That sounds fine. I will be there tomorrow. What time did you say?"

There was a soft moaning sound as Dave released the built-up tension of him missing Emily in his office.

"Mr. Banks?"

Julia's voice refocused his attention back to their conversation about lunch. Dave cleared his vocal cords, not once but twice. Not hearing the question Julia had asked, Dave responded quickly, trying to end the call, not because he was embarrassed about what just happened. He needed to start working on his plan to close his practice in Philadelphia and get credentialed to practice in South Carolina. "Well then, I will see you tomorrow at noon. Have a good day."

Chapter 18

mily's heart sinks and she rushes for the front yard where Kyndall and Pearl remain deep in conversation.

"Kyndall, may I have a moment of your time?" Urgency colors Emily's voice.

Pearl raises an eyebrow. It's not like Emily to interrupt, let alone interrupt to *request* a conversation with Kyndall. Yet, here she is rushing toward her. "It was nice talking to you, Mrs. Graham."

Kyndall responds, "Likewise," while brushing a piece of hair off her face. "Hi, Emily, what's up?"

Emily marvels at the casual response, as if directed at a best friend, not a woman she had spent the past half hour chastising.

Emily's voice is shaky as she explains, "I just received ten text messages with photos of Brendon and an unidentified young lady in uncompromising positions…with drug paraphernalia."

She unlocks her phone and clicks on the text message icon and hands it to Kyndall, who peruses the photos without a single word, but her heavy breathing and throat clearing betray her. Her lips purse as she views the last photo. "Please send me each and every one."

"Of course. Should I call Brendon?"

"No! I will take care of this. Stay by the phone and I will update you once I know something."

Emily is taken aback by Kyndall's snap, but she agrees.

What Kyndall doesn't tell Emily is that she knows exactly where Brendon is. One photo of Brendon and his "date" depicts the skyline of downtown Center City, where she and Brendon share an apartment. Kyndall gives Emily a kiss on the cheek. "Everything will be okay. I will take care of the chaos…as usual."

Emily is shocked to find herself embracing her mother-in-law. Kyndall pats her back as she reciprocates, as if to shake off the twinge of shame she feels for the way she treated Emily earlier. "It was for her own good," she reminds herself. *Emily needed to hear it, even though it was hurtful; Emily needed to snap back to reality, our reality. We are a family that sticks together and helps each other when they are down. That is all I was trying to do with Emily, help shape her vision of the future the way I see it. Brendon and Emily both deserve to live in the White House, and they will get there one way or the other.*

Kyndall breaks away from Emily's embrace and gently places her right hand on Emily's face. "I will make this all better."

Emily smiles halfheartedly and Kyndall removes her hand from Emily's face and searches for her keys. She uses the unlock feature on her key to open the door as she walks toward the car. When she opens the door, she steals a final glance at Emily disappearing into the house. She sighs. Her son's mistakes are destroying Emily, and she can't let that happen. She promised Doris that she would take care of Emily, and she always upholds her end of any deal, no matter the consequences.

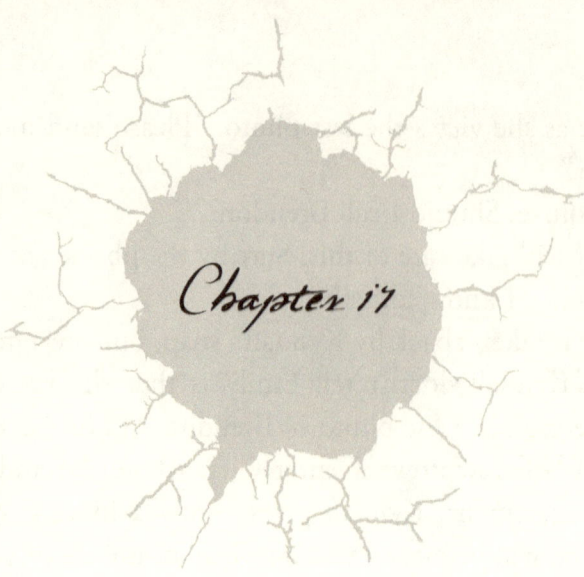

Chapter 17

Emily walks back into the house, knowing Kyndall will handle the situation with Brendon and the unidenti- fied young lady. Young lady? Emily snorts. *That's rich.* The girl in the photo is probably an escort just like the other women he met when he tells her he must "work late." Brendon came up with the "work late" code after they went through months of counseling and Brendon professed that he had come to grips with his sexual addiction and was ready to channel his energy toward his career and family. He stayed on track for six months before invent- ing work trips that didn't exist and extending his hours that last Friday night into Saturday. Emily knew, then, that he had fallen back into his old ways. This was when she consulted an attorney to learn about her options.

The secret meetings with the attorney tore her up inside be- cause she didn't have anyone she could talk to about what she was going through emotionally. Just discussing a divorce with her attorney brought on panic attacks. The worst one occurred on the day she drove to pick up the divorce papers that were finally drawn up. She had reached the parking lot and pulled in a space near the front door of her attorney's office. The car was in park and Emily had turned off the ignition. Her hands had started to shake and had become increasingly wet while perspiration gushed down her face. She couldn't breathe and started to unbutton the top three buttons of her white lace, high-collared blouse to keep from choking. She coughed twice. Her throat was closing, so she coughed again.

Mr. Martin, one of the partners in the law firm, noticed Emily as he walked toward his car after meeting with Marsha Watson, another lawyer in the office. Mr. Martin knocked on the window of the driver's side. "Hi, are you okay?" Emily didn't acknowledge hearing him, so he knocked again. "Are you okay?" Still no answer from Emily. He dropped his briefcase and pulled out his cell phone and dialed 911. "There's a client of my law firm having a medical emergency in her car. Her car door is locked and I can't get in to assist her."

"Sir, what is your name?"

"Mark Martin."

"Mark, my name is Beth. I want you to take a deep breath and we will get through this together." The calmness of Beth's voice caused Mark's anxiety level to decrease as he complied with her requests.

"Mark, what's your address?"

He gave the dispatcher the address of his law practice and added, "You need to hurry—she doesn't look good."

"I have dispatched the local police and fire departments; they should be there within the next several minutes. I want you to stay on the line with me. What do you see in the car? Do you see food that she may be choking on?"

"No, I don't see any food. Is there something I can do, like break the window or open the door? I have never done anything like that before but I will try."

"Mark, I want you to stay calm. The fire department's estimated arrival time is less than thirty seconds."

As the dispatcher was speaking, a police officer arrived on the scene along with the fire department.

"Beth, both the fire department and local police are here now."

"Mark, thank you for the update. I hope you have a good day." Beth released the line and moved to her next emergency call.

"Sir, please step aside," said the firefighter named Frank; his name was displayed on the right side of his fire suit. Frank approached the vehicle to find the young lady in the car in distress. He reached for the automatic center punch, placed it on the right corner of the window, and pushed inward. The glass immediately shattered, creating a hole the size of a quarter where the tool was placed. He took his gloved right hand and placed it in the hole, pulling the glass toward him while trying to avoid getting it in the car. He unlocked the door to find Emily conscious, but unaware of the events that had taken place. Frank carried her to the sidewalk. "Ma'am, can you hear me?"

Emily responded, "Yes."

"What's your name?" Frank shined a bright light into her eyes.

By this time, EMS was on the scene. The paramedics lifted Emily's arms and carefully placed her on the stretcher to transport her to the ambulance. One, two, three, they lifted the stretcher so Emily could be examined by the team. They checked her heart rate and gave her some oxygen to smooth her choppy breathing. Once Emily's breathing had returned to normal, the paramedics asked, "What happened here today?"

"My attorney called to tell me my divorce papers were ready to be picked up and I felt my chest tighten sitting in the car."

"It sounds as though you were experiencing a panic attack. We can transport you to the hospital for a full examination, just to be on the safe side."

"No, I don't need to go to the hospital. I have experienced something similar in the past."

"If you decide that you don't want to go to the hospital, then you must sign a release that you refused treatment."

Emily asked Susan, the paramedic, for the release form and signed to acknowledge that she refused treatment. She then got up from the stretcher and exited the back of the ambulance to walk up the sidewalk to the attorney's office and do what she never thought she would do—pick up divorce papers to end her marriage.

Emily's thoughts bring her back to her current situation with Brendon. Her iPhone is in sleep mode, so she hits the oval button at the bottom and slides it to the right to enter her password. She has one missed call. Upon retrieving her voicemail, she hears Julia's voice on the other end. The excitement that Emily experiences makes her hands tremble and sweat, not the same symptoms she gets when she's having a panic attack. Her head swims and she giggles, like a young teenage girl in love. Julia mentions in her message that Doris found her on Facebook and reached out to her a couple of hours ago, so she thought that she would take the chance and call. She left her number for Emily to call her back.

After all these years, Julia and Emily had lost contact with one another, but they had been very close at Temple. Emily smiles as she recalls their plans to conquer the world after graduation.

Julia had been a university ambassador for freshman orientation and gave tours to small groups of incoming new students. She had an air about her that projected confidence, not arrogance. She was someone who was beautiful, but didn't realize that she could capture attention simply by walking into a room. Even that first day, Julia's smile had created butterflies in Emily's stomach.

Emily, on the other hand, had been categorized by her high school classmates as a nerd. The name-calling hadn't bothered her; she was oblivious to what others did and said. Instead, she concentrated on her school work. She wanted to make her mother proud by receiving awards and excelling in the classroom. She succeeded at this, but failed miserably at developing social skills and a positive self-image, which created a situation where she was extremely shy when it came to boys. She couldn't look them in the eyes, even when they were standing in front of her. Her low self-esteem came from the prescription thickness of the glasses she wore, the glasses that her classmates called Coca-Cola bottles.

When Emily was in middle school, she started to look more mature, with her breasts growing into a C cup and her hips beginning to curve; when she entered her freshman year of high school, she was more developed than the other girls in her class, which didn't help Emily's body image. She would find herself wearing clothes that hid or covered her breasts, which just added to the overall attention she was drawing to herself.

Emily thought that was all behind her and she was ready to start her new life as a college student. Even though she was smart and could apply herself to any program she put her mind to, she decided to pursue a liberal arts degree. During roll call at the beginning and the end of the tour, Emily blushed each time Julia said her name.

It was the final day of the exciting two-day orientation, and Julia had them all line up to give room assignments. Emily remembered feeling just as she had in high school when teams were chosen during physical education. She was always the last person to join whatever team was being assigned. Volleyball...basketball... It didn't matter in high school, and it didn't matter at that moment. Emily's smile faded and the excitement she felt about starting over began to dissipate. All the students who toured with her over the weekend had all buddied up and there wasn't anyone left but Emily. She approached the table with her eyes focused on an imaginary spot on the floor of the gym. She told Julia that she knew that all the room assignments were taken and her parents couldn't afford a private room, so she wasn't sure what she should do.

"Emily, Emily, it's okay. I have a roommate for you. I will be your roommate in the fall."

Instantly, the butterflies in Emily's stomach began to flutter with renewed vigor. *I am the winner out of everyone here today: I finally got first choice.* It took a few moments for Emily to lift her eyes from the floor to Julia's smiling face and mutter, "Thank you."

Over the next three years, Emily had followed Julia around like a puppy. Julia had showed her how to accentuate all the qualities that the bullies criticized her for in high school, and thus, Emily adored her. More importantly, Julia had worked on Emily's overall self-image internally and externally by first recommending that she let her hair grow out and not to chop off her bangs. The pageboy look was dated, and Emily needed a fresh look. Over the course of several months, Emily's hair grew and she experimented with many different styles, including updos at the salon. Emily expressed that she wanted to get in shape and wanted Julia to teach her the discipline in running; she went from fifteen minutes of nearly falling to the ground even in a very slow trot to running four miles a day, sixteen miles a week. Emily felt strong and confident. She even changed her major to business to clearly define the path she wanted to take. She wanted to start her own marketing firm.

Julia…well, she had known what she wanted to do since she could speak… She wanted to be an engineer. She took the tough classes and, each summer, had internships with the most prestigious firms, solidifying her career. Emily found Julia's confidence sexy and wanted to gain that kind of control; she neither felt sexy nor had confidence. She wasn't sure what to make of those feelings. Was it love? She didn't know. She felt…something between them, but how could it be love? After all, she had never felt it, nor could she fathom being in a relationship with a woman. How could she? She was dating Brendon Graham.

The night of Julia's graduation brought Emily and Brendon closer. Emily stared into Brendon's eyes. "Kiss me." Brendon and Emily shared a strong kiss. Emily opened her eyes and saw Julia staring at them, but she shrugged it off. She was tired of trying to figure it out…and, after all, if Julia truly cared for her, why did she kiss Samantha? She forced herself to block out the disappointment she felt by pressing herself against Brendon's warm body. They walked back to the parking garage where Brendon opened the passenger door of his white Maserati. She quickly wiped a tear from her eye so Brendon wouldn't see her cry as she thought about how Julia had disappointed her. He opened the driver side door and slid into the seat that fit him like a glove. He revved the engine and exited the parking garage.

Emily stayed with Brendon the entire weekend and returned to the dorm that she shared with Julia to find all of Julia's belongings gone. No note, nothing, Julia was gone from her life forever. Emily chose Brendon by default so her heart wouldn't hurt as much. Brendon was available and was going to make something of himself, so Emily latched onto him. Within a year after graduation, they married.

The company Emily interned with throughout college hired her on as a marketing assistant. She worked hard for three years and received her first promotion as an associate in the marketing department; at the same time, she visited the doctor and was told she was six weeks pregnant. Emily and Brendon discussed starting a family, but she just wasn't ready, not now that her career was escalating and she enjoyed the work she was doing. Emily continued to work and refused to tell her manager, Martini, she was pregnant. She was fully pregnant, meaning her belly reached her destination two minutes before she could catch up.

One day, Martini called Emily into the office. "Emily, you

have never discussed with me that you were pregnant and your plans to take maternity leave. I am concerned not only for you, but for your baby that you take the time you need."

Emily smiled at Martini; not only was she her boss but a dear friend. "I know. I feel as though my career is just starting, and now Brendon and I are starting a family. It appears everything is happening so fast. I wanted to at least work for the next several years to establish my name in the field of marketing and then slow my pace down." Emily rubbed her belly. "Ouch, I am going to have a little soccer player. The babies are kicking."

"Babies...? Emily, you and Brendon are having twins?"

"Martini, I am so sorry. I have been out of it throughout the course of my pregnancy and haven't shared any of this with you. Yes, we are expecting twins."

"I am so happy for the both of you. Now I really am concerned that you request the time you need for leave."

With a warm smile, Emily assured Martini she would submit her maternity leave paperwork first thing the next morning. The arm of the chair offered her support as she struggled to get up. Another strong kick from the baby stopped Emily in her tracks and she reached for the chair arm to steady herself. Her right hand moved toward her belly and rubbed the spot to calm her little one. "Are you okay?" Martini asked as she moved toward Emily, one hand on her back and the other on her arm.

"Yeah, I will be fine." Emily brushed Martini's hand away from her. She didn't like to be fussed over, especially after she had carried the twins and worked forty-plus hours every week. No time to be treated like an invalid. Emily wobbled down the hall toward her office and closed the door.

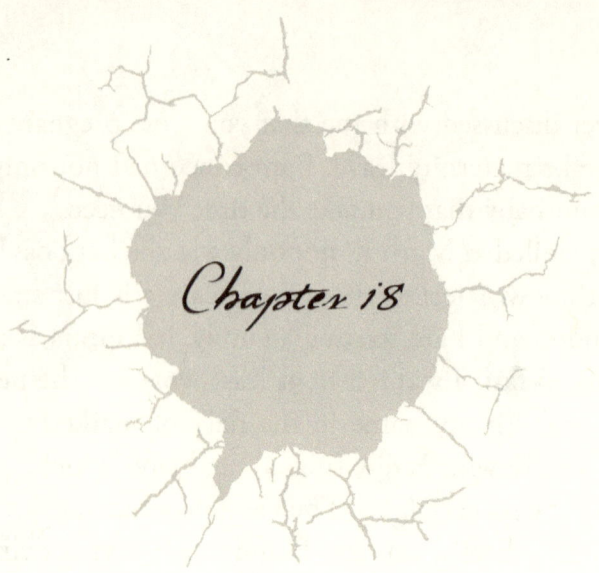

Chapter 18

Even though Emily wanted to work until her due date, her body had other plans. The same night she and Martini discussed her submitting her maternity leave paperwork, Emily was rushed to the hospital, where she delivered two healthy twins, Madison and Connor.

After the birth of the twins Emily wanted to go back to work but Kyndall insisted that "a good mother stays at home with her children." She wanted to be a good mother, so she decided to stay home for two years. Two years became three, and three became four…and so on. When the twins turned eight years old, Emily gradually went back to work as a marketing consultant, part time at first, but soon transitioned to a full-time work schedule. She had the flexibility to work out of the home, so she didn't have to be away from the kids.

Madison and Connor took Emily's thoughts back to the birth of her first son. Brendon had lived off campus and the two of them had fun when they were together; he made her laugh. They were inseparable all throughout college. They had an active sexual relationship, which resulted in a pregnancy during Emily's junior year. Emily found out she was pregnant during the winter quarter, when she was five months. Brendon had been great; he stood by Emily the entire time of the pregnancy. She stayed with Brendon until the baby, Ian, was born. Ian had made his entrance into the world a little earlier than expected. Emily had gotten up at 6:00 a.m. on Tuesday, August 4th to go to the bathroom, which wasn't unusual because Ian was always sitting on her bladder. She headed to the bathroom and as she approached the door, water gushed down her leg. "Brendon!" Brendon had stirred in the bed, but didn't get up. "Brendon!" yelled Emily the second time. Brendon's body bolted up. "What? What? Are you okay?" He gasped when he saw Emily doubled over, and his brain told him to rush toward her. He swung his legs out of the bed too fast and fell clumsily on the floor, hitting his head on the nightstand. They were both a mess; Brendon clutched his forehead as he walked toward Emily, still doubled over on the floor. Even though she was in pain, she still found the humor in seeing Brendon fall.

"Are you okay?" Brendon asked.

"Brendon, get my bag—my water broke."

"What?" He looked down to see the puddle of water on the bathroom floor. "Oh, shit, Em, we are having a baby."

Gregory, Brendon's roommate, had come over and asked, "What's going on?"

"Emily is having the baby."

Gregory went into director mode and started to bark orders to the group. "Brendon, go get dressed and I will get the SUV; we will have more room in my car than yours." Brendon began to dress while Gregory sprinted to the front door, snatching Emily's suitcase from behind the chair. Everyone started to move and do their part. Gregory pulled up in front of the apartment with flashing blinkers. Brendon ushered Emily toward the car and helped her in the backseat so she could stretch out. While in the car

Brendon called Emily's doctor's office to let the service know that she was in labor and they were on their way to the hospital. "Tell them the contractions are fifteen minutes apart," yelled Gregory from the front seat. Brendon relayed the message and the service said that they would let the doctor know. Within five minutes Dr. Adams had called Brendon back and told him that he was on the way to the hospital.

Gregory pulled up to the emergency room door, parking the car so close that the sensor to the automatic door kept the doors open. He jumped out of the car and got a wheelchair; he and Brendon each took Emily by an arm, gently placing her in the chair. "Brendon, I will park the car and be right back. What floor is maternity?" The confused, dazed look Brendon gave Gregory signaled his shock of all the events of the night. "Never mind, I will find you," Gregory said in a huff. He walked back to the car to find a parking space marked "visitor."

Brendon had Emily checked in and heading toward her room. Once she was settled in her room, the contractions were minutes apart and Emily had dilated enough that the doctor could see the crown of the baby's head. The doctor rushed Emily to the operating room and asked Brendon to scrub in as well. Brendon took his place near Emily's shoulders and held her hand as she started to scream. He didn't know what else to do or say, so he told Emily it was going to be okay.

Emily refused the epidural, but thought differently as the pain became unbearable. At that point, there wasn't anything the doctor could give her and they asked Emily to give one hard push. Emily pushed and she heard her baby boy, Ian, cry. The nurse took Ian and started to clean him up. He was returned to his parents swaddled, a perfect little package for them to marvel at. Emily carefully studied Ian. She looked him over with a guarded stare from his full head of dark brown hair to the shape of his button nose. All features could resemble Brendon, but she wasn't entirely convinced that Ian looked enough like Brendon to say without hesitation that he was the father. She was glad that they had decided to give the baby up for adoption. It was mostly her idea. She had to do a lot of convincing and urging Brendon that both their families would be upset if they dropped out of school to care for a small baby. Brendon eventually broke down and agreed, but it took many months for him to change his mind.

For Emily, it was an easy decision. She didn't want to have to look at the child every day and remember the heinous act. Emily had a dark secret: she had been raped by her college professor, Mr. Banks. Emily had been sexting with Brendon all afternoon, and planned for Brendon to come and see her in the room. She had left the door open so that Brendon could enter without calling her. The door opened and she thought that it was Brendon who entered her from behind. Her pleasure turned to horror when she caught a glimpse of her psychology instructor's reflection in the mirror and he quickly dressed and exited the room. Emily lay there unable to understand why Mr. Banks would come into her room and violate her in that way. She got up and sat in the shower for two hours, scrubbing furiously to get the scent of him off her. She was torn in reporting the incident to campus police, but decided that no one would believe her, so she kept the secret to herself. The next day, Emily withdrew from class and planned to never see him again. She would take the class over at a local community college or take it with another instructor.

Emily panicked when she missed her period and again when the doctor confirmed she was pregnant. She tried to keep hope alive by convincing herself that the baby was Brendon's, but the math suggested otherwise. She was too far along to not let Brendon know that she was pregnant.

When Brendon heard the news, he smiled and kissed her on the forehead. "We will be great parents," he whispered.

Emily cried when Brendon spoke the words that were meant

to be an affirmation of their solid relationship, but couldn't help but think that she could never raise a child who brought back so many painful memories. "Brendon, we can't have this baby."

"It's going to be all right. I know my mother will be upset but I will handle her."

"No, Brendon!" yelled Emily. "We can't have this baby." She pulled away from Brendon and ran into the bathroom to be alone. Brendon walked to the door to beg Emily to come out, but decided against it. Emily needed more time to think about her pregnancy so she turned and walked toward the bedroom and closed the door.

Both Emily and Brendon had the opportunity to spend time with Ian before Yolanda, the case worker from social services, entered the room to take him. Emily handed Ian to Brendon and she turned her back to the three of them, crying softly. Each tear vanished on the softness of the cotton pillowcase. Brendon used his index finger and touched Ian's nose. The little boy kicked his legs and arms in the air in response. Brendon got a kick out of seeing his baby boy so happy and he touched the baby again, receiving the same reaction. Brendon used the back of his hand to wipe the flowing tears from both sides of his cheeks. "I am ready." Brendon turned and handed the baby over to Yolanda.

"I know this is hard," Yolanda began, but before she could complete her sentence, Brendon told her, "Thank you, have a good evening." Yolanda knew it was her cue that the family no longer wanted her there, so she took Ian and closed the door behind her.

Chapter 19

mily stared out the window of Brendon's apartment, pensively thinking about Ian. *Where is he? Is he with a good family?* She knows that she and Brendon agreed to give Ian up for adoption but her heart ached with regret.

The fall semester started and Emily was healed enough physically to go back to school, but emotionally she wasn't ready to socialize with anyone. She stayed a few more weeks at Brendon's apartment. Brendon was very caring and tended to Emily's every need, although he, too, was dealing with mixed emotions. Brendon turned to alcohol and heroin to numb his pain. He began to walk through life without feeling because he didn't want to have to deal with the empty hole in his heart. Emily watched Brendon from afar, not knowing how to help him because, she, too, was hurting.

Emily moved closer to Brendon after he snorted the last line of heroin and pulled his head to her chest and quietly murmured, "I am sorry." They both cried softly in each other's arms as Emily kissed his forehead.

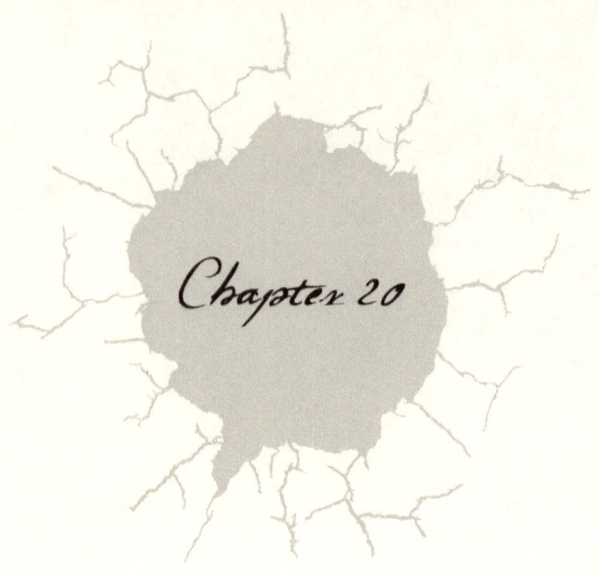

Chapter 20

Kyndall arrives at the apartment and takes the stairs to the tenth floor to avoid anyone in the lobby and the security cameras. She knew where they all were and the angle of each, and either turned her back to them or managed to hold her head to the right or left, depending on where the camera was located, to avoid it catching her face.

Kyndall reaches the tenth floor and walks to the far end of the hallway to apartment 1035, the last apartment on the right. She knocks rather loudly on the door to wake the dead or at least to get Brendon's attention. Brendon looks through the peephole. "Mother, go home."

"Open this door immediately; I know you have someone here with you."

"Mother, this isn't the deal; I can have my privacy when we aren't scheduled to use the apartment."

"Brendon, are you crazy? Stop talking and open this door, immediately."

Brendon obeys his mother and cracks the door only slightly. "What do you want?" he barks.

"Do you understand that your prostitute sent Emily pictures of the two of you?"

"No, she couldn't have. I followed the protocol of locking up all electronic devices when guests arrive."

"My stupid son, have you ever thought that the whore used your phone to take the pictures and sent them to your wife?"

"Mother, don't call her a whore. Her name is Catherine and she is an escort, not a whore."

"Are you kidding me right now? Just because you pay the escort service and not the girl doesn't mean she isn't a hooker. I swear, sometimes you are so naïve. I guess I should make all the presidential decisions while you sit and look pretty."

Brendon gives his mother a stern look. "You can only rob a man of his manhood so many times before he loathes you. Why do you think Dad spends more time away from home than with you? You run every man away from you with your sharp, spear-like tongue. You pushed Dad into the arms of another woman."

Kyndall has heard just about enough from her son and his smart mouth. "You listen here; no one does anything in this family without my knowing and approving it. I chose the mistress for your father; she met my approval and I set it up. So, before you tell me what a bad mother I am, I want to remind you what I did for you to save your marriage. The sex clubs and prostitutes hindered you from performing sexually with your wife, and I would give you sexual pleasure to get you through the rough patches of your marriage. I am the only one in your life who will do any and everything it takes to ensure you are happy. Do you remember the night of the masquerade party? I never knew it was you behind the mask, but when you pulled up your mask, I wanted to stop. I couldn't have sex with my son, but you insisted. There wasn't anything between the two of us, except our naked bodies. I yelled no, stop, this is your mother. You replied that you knew and fantasized what it would be like to be with me. I didn't know, but you knew."

"Oh, Mother, you act as though you didn't like it. Why keep the apartment if you didn't want to keep having sex with your son?"

"Brendon, I didn't come here to have this conversation with you. Where is the whore? I mean Catherine."

"She's in the next room, asleep."

Kyndall reaches in her purse to find her phone and shoves it in his chest.

"Did Emily see these pictures?"

"Yes," snaps Kyndall. "She sent them to me and that's how I knew where to come."

"Oh no, Mother, what should I do? Emily will never forgive me. I need to keep my wife and family."

"That's the first smart thing you have said since I arrived. While you've been getting your freak on, your wife had an attorney draw up divorce papers. The American people won't elect a president who is divorced."

Salty, warm tears stream down Brendon's eyes into his mouth as he licks his chapped upper lip. Kyndall gets a headache from watching Brendon pace back and forth, running his hand through his freshly cut hair. In a low, panicked whisper Brendon begs, "Mother, how can I make this right with Emily? What can I do? I will do anything."

"We will work everything out with Emily later. How much does the girl know? Does she know who you are?"

Brendon shakes his head no.

"She used my alias, Andy, but said that I didn't look like an Andy. She said I looked like someone she's seen on television recently." Brendon continues to pace back and forth.

Catherine stirs in the bed; the sheets crinkle as she moves her body from side to side, reaching for Andy or whatever his name is. The place where his body used to be is cold. Catherine stretches and opens her eyes to find her lover not lying beside her. "Where're those voices coming from?" Catherine forces her relaxed body to rise. She stretches long and places one leg at a time to the floor. "Who is the female he is talking to? Is it Andy's wife?" Catherine gingerly turns the knob with her left hand while using her right hand to brace any sound the door may make to hear the conversation coming from the next room. The door is only ajar enough for her to view the room from the right side. The woman in the room is older, she looks old enough to perhaps be his mother, but that's strange. From the frequency of the text messages and phone calls in the call log, she thought his wife would have come to confront him, not this older woman. "Who is she?" Catherine stands at the door, listening to find out more information on this mysterious woman. *What? Did he just call her Mother? Why would his mother come to his apartment when he had company? How did she know I was here?* There are so many questions, but such little time. She needs to figure out who is the woman in the other room. *This guy must be someone important. Who is he?*

The argument between the two of them grows heated at some points. She thinks the older lady called him President. *No, that can't be true; the current President is African-American. Maybe she said he's running for the presidency, but this isn't an election year. Who is he?* Still eyeing Andy, she hears him get emotional when the older lady says that Emily knew… *What does Emily know? Ah, Emily must be his wife.* Catherine's body jolts straight up and she stops playing junior detective when she hears the older lady say, "We must get rid of her. We will make her death look like an overdose."

Get rid of who, me?! Catherine's eyes open wide and her right hand slaps her mouth to hold back any scream that is forthcoming. Catherine is still high with the booze and drugs, but knows she's in life-or-death trouble. Her heart sinks. Her eyes dart around the room, looking for a way to escape. It takes her all of twenty seconds to decide she can't open the bedroom door and walk straight into the arms of her killers. Opening the door to the balcony is the only option. Then what? Jump off the balcony? Catherine knows that if she wants to see her mother again she must move now or it will literally be never. She gently closes the bedroom door and looks around the room for her clothes. Catherine finds her bra and fastens it and turns the bra so the breast cups were now in front, allowing her to slip her arms through the straps. Her black-and-white dress from White House Black Market is draped haphazardly on the chair; she slips it over her head, glad she didn't wear the other dress with the zipper that she had laid out before changing her mind at the last minute. Catherine turns to the bed searching under the covers for her underwear, but gives up. Corpses don't wear underwear in the medical examiner's office. She scrambles for her purse and shoes. In truth, she could leave the purse, but she spent a fortune on her red-bottom Christian Louboutin's. She doesn't care who is chasing her; she won't leave them behind. She interlocks them by the strap and opens the sliding glass door in the bedroom to the balcony. A unique feature of this apartment is the two entrances to the balcony, one from the bedroom and one from the living area.

Why did I take this job? Catherine was only home to visit her mother, but when Brandy, one of the girls she became friends with, asked if she would cover for her so she could spend time with her boyfriend before he went off to basic training at Fort Jackson the next day, Catherine couldn't say no. Plus she needed the extra money to pay for a home health-care provider for her sick mother. *This is what I get for being nice.* She grimaces.

The warm breeze from the balcony calms Catherine's nerves for only a minute. "Where in the hell do I go from here?" Catherine ponders a strategy, which is no strategy at all because they are ten floors up. *Option one, I can balance myself on the edge of the rail and walk from apartment to apartment like a tightrope at* the circus. But there is a point that the rail stops and I would have to jump to the next apartment where the rail starts again. I have seen this stunt done many times on television; it was as ridiculous then as it is now. Plus, I am afraid of heights. The second option is to jump, which isn't a real option because I would die on impact, and if I had a death wish I could have stayed in the bedroom and let Norman Bates and his mother kill me by making it look like a drug overdose. Option three is to try to talk my way out of the situation.*

Catherine takes a slow, deep breath and starts to cry; each idea is more stupid than the first. She paces back and forth to stimulate thoughts on how to get out of this jam. Catherine stops. The talking in the living room has stopped. She stands on the side of the door that leads to the living room and sees no one. She decides to wing it. *Option four is my best bet; make a run for it.* Catherine turns the knob on the door and enters the living room. She hurries on the tips of her toes to the front door.

Catherine reflects to the events of the evening. *I am glad that I took the pictures on the balcony earlier, because the door leading to the balcony from the living area would not have been opened and my luck would have run out.* She opens the door and sprints down the hall. In her peripheral vision, she sees Brendon running after her. She takes the stairs because there's no time to wait for the elevator. Brendon runs to the end of the hall and loses Catherine in the foot chase. He decides to head back to the apartment. It would be unacceptable for someone to see the senator for the State of Pennsylvania running after a young lady down the halls of the apartment building.

Huffing and puffing, Brendon opens the door of the apartment to find his mother on the phone; he assumes she is speaking with Gregory, Brendon's roommate from college. After graduation, Gregory and Brendon remained friends, hanging out at least once a month for drinks. Not that Gregory didn't mind hanging out more, but once a month was all the spare time either one of them had, with Brendon's career and his family. Gregory had a family of his own with his wife, Amy, and three beautiful daughters—Elizabeth (ten), Mona (eight), and Stephanie (two). Greg and Amy thought they were done changing diapers after Mona, but when Amy found out she was pregnant with Stephanie they were both delighted to have the pitter patter of little feet running around again. It was as though Stephanie was their first. Greg named the Graham clan—Emily, Brendon, Kyndall, and Wellington—as godparents, as he couldn't think of a better family to raise their daughters if something ever happened to him and Amy. It took Amy some time to warm up to the idea of Kyndall raising their daughters or even visiting them; there was something about her that Amy just didn't trust. Gregory never discussed how he could provide an extravagant lifestyle, but she knew that every time Kyndall called Gregory, a large amount of money was deposited into the account, anywhere from $10,000 to $20,000. Amy wasn't sure why there was such a huge range in the amount being deposited other than the sophistication level of the "favor" Kyndall asked of Gregory. In any event, Amy had her doubts about Kyndall and the motives behind what she did.

Amy turned a blind eye to the large amount of money being deposited into her and Gregory's account because she and Greg were in student loan debt. Greg gave up a job with a large software company to take a part-time help desk job at a local IT company to pursue his PhD in Information Systems with an emphasis in Networking. Amy majored in Early Childhood Education and worked as a teacher at a local high school, until their second daughter was born. Gregory and Amy decided that it was more practical and cost effective for Amy to stay at home with their daughters than for the two of them to balance dual careers and all that came with that, including paying the extra expense for daycare and deciding who was going to pick the children up from school. It made more sense for Amy to stay at home; Gregory earned more money and he had the flexibility to help Amy out around the house because of his work schedule. Money was tight, but they managed by buying just what they needed when they needed it. Kyndall helped the family out by offering Greg odd jobs here and there and the couple's debt problems started to diminish. The payouts after each job grew from $1,000 to the sum of $10,000 per job. After Gregory proved he was loyal to Kyndall, she depended on him more and more, from general IT questions to hacking into someone's personal computer. Because Kyndall's needs varied, Greg became her go-to person for non-IT-related needs, which made Greg more and more valuable to Kyndall. As Brendon became more powerful, Kyndall needed him more and more.

Six months ago, Kyndall called him to meet her in DC at the Loews Madison, where Brendon had had a wild night in the penthouse suite with an escort by the name of Candy, who Stella provided. Candy came by the penthouse dressed in Elie Tahari's Alicia pleated chiffon black dress with a matching leather envelope purse and the Harpers stiletto in black. The small diamond stud earrings were a simple touch to such an elegant outfit, with the tight bun pulled back to the nape of her neck. Candy greeted Brendon with her right hand on her hip and the left hand above her head holding the purse, leaning on the door frame.

Brendon opened the door. "You must be Candy?"

"I am," Candy responded with a sly, sexy smile.

"It's nice to meet you, Candy, I'm Andy," Brendon replied. "May I please take any electronic devices you have? It is one of my policies not to share our evening on social media."

Candy opened the envelope purse and pulled out her iPhone and extended it to him. Brendon reached for the phone and moved to the bedroom and put his code into the safe. He reappeared. "What else do you have in that little purse of yours?"

"Really! Are we going to do this? I gave you my phone!" screamed Candy at the top of her lungs.

Brendon took the purse without answering Candy's question and dumped all its contents on the coffee table. He examined all the items; nothing seemed unusual. Clinique Stay-Matte Sheer Pressed Powder; Butter Shine Lipstick Ambrosia; Dentyne Winter Chill sugar-free gum; Bank of America debit card with the name Alina Ivanovich. *She is Russian,* thought Brendon.

"Since you are searching, you need to make sure I don't have any electronic devices under my dress." Alina unzipped her dress, and gravity pulled it to the floor, exposing her voluptuous body. She was wearing nothing but her diamond stud earrings. "You need to search in every nook and cranny, as the Americans say."

Brendon chuckled. "Come here."

He loved her accent and would have to request her the next time he was in DC, if things worked out. After several hours of lovemaking, room service arrived promptly at 7:00 p.m. Brendon had arranged a dinner of steak and lobster; green beans with shallots and mushrooms; two baked sweet potatoes; and a side salad for the two of them. The dessert of choice was strawberries and cream with two bottles of champagne. Brendon pushed the room service cart to the balcony and they ate dinner under the stars, holding hands and gazing into each other's eyes. Brendon drained the champagne. He licked the mouth of the bottle before throwing it to the floor. He turned to Alina. "Do you want to have some real fun?"

"What do you mean real fun? I thought we are having the fun," Alina said in her broken English.

"No, I mean some real fun," Brendon said. "I have some smack I picked up this afternoon. Do you want to try some?"

"What is the smack?"

"Smack is the street name for heroin. Do you want to try some with me?"

Alina usually stayed away from drugs, but not that day. She liked this guy and wanted to see him soon, off the clock. If doing a little "smack" would get her closer to him, she was game.

"Sure, I will do the smack."

Brendon disappeared in the next room and brought back a tiny bag of snow-white powder, a plate, and the square door key. He emptied the bag on to the plate and used the door key to make straight lines to evenly divide the heroin for easy consumption. Tap, tap, tap came from the other side of the door. "Who is it?" Brendon said in a distracted and uninterested tone. He licked his lips as he divided the last line, his nostrils flaring in anticipation of the euphoric sensation of the heroin brimming throughout his body. The tapping got louder, which caused Brendon to become more agitated. "Who is it?"

Alina replied, "They say the room service; did you not hear them the first time?"

Brendon jumped up from the chair to answer the door. He walked halfway toward the door, but had a second thought and walked back to where Alina was sitting. "Don't start without me. I will be right back." He kissed her on the forehead. "I will be right there," yelled Brendon as he walked toward the front door, finding his slacks on the way and putting them on before opening the door.

Juan, the young man who brought room service earlier, emerged from the other side of the door with an ice bucket of champagne and two champagne flutes. "Hello, here's your champagne," said Juan, thinking, *Qué te tomó tanto tiempo*, as he gave Brendon a dirty look. With a half-smile, Brendon pulled out his wallet and gave Juan two crisp twenty-dollar bills. Juan extended his hand. "Thank you, sir." Before Brendon closed the door, Juan muttered, *Mi tiempo es tan valioso como el suyo rico hombre*, shaking his head as he walked down the hall toward the elevator.

"Alina, I have our special juice! We can continue to celebrate!" shouted Brendon from the living room as he made his way back to the balcony. "Honey, here I come." There was silence from the area where Brendon left her. Brendon stepped onto the balcony and his eyes took him to Alina; his hands released his grip on the ice bucket, and all its contents crashed to the floor. Shards of glass exploded in all directions. Brendon found Alina convulsing in the chaise, white bubbles dribbling down both sides of her mouth. Brendon stood looking at his lover, and forced himself to scan the scene. There were only two lines of smack left on the plate; Alina had snorted five lines, the white powder residue on the rim of her nose.

The poor woman. Her first time doing drugs, and he had led her to disaster. Tears started to stream down his cheeks as he paced the floor as he often did when he was in a situation that troubled him. Brendon retrieved his cell phone from the coffee table and dialed the only person who knew how to get him out of this mess.

Chapter 21

Kyndall picked up the phone on the third ring and saw from the caller ID that it was Brendon. She knew he was in trouble for him to call her at this hour.

"Mother, something tragic has happened and I don't know what to do."

Kyndall braced herself. Each time Brendon called crying, his actions were more heinous. Even though Kyndall was aggravated with him, she dug deep to find her motherly instinct to respond gently to him. "Sweetheart, you know you can tell me anything. What happened?" This was the only response she could think to give. He needed to tell her what he did so she could start once again fixing the destruction.

"I was with a young lady tonight and she overdosed on heroin."

Kyndall thought, *Same problem but different girl. Hmm, I know the young lady he is referring to is an escort.* She could read between the lines. "Are you okay? Did you take any of the drugs?"

"I am okay, but I was paying room service and when I came back to the balcony she was foaming at the mouth and convulsing."

"Where are you? Are you at the apartment in Philly?"

"No, I am in DC at the Loews Madison."

"I am on my way. Don't leave the room, not even for ice. I need you to work on getting yourself sober by showering and drinking plenty of coffee. I don't need you high because we are going to have to figure out what to do with the prostitute."

"Mother, she's an escort."

"Brendon, don't start with me with your play on words. She is what she is." There was silence from Brendon. "Leave everything the way it is so we can assess how to clean up this mess."

"Okay, Mother" was the last response between Kyndall and Brendon until he heard a knock on the door.

After Kyndall got off the phone with Brendon she immediately called Gregory and told him what was happening; she needed him to assist with a situation. It took both Kyndall and Gregory two hours and thirty minutes to drive from Philly to DC. Gregory knew that situations which occurred in the middle of the night were complicated and usually someone ended up dead. Gregory had grabbed his gear, kissed Amy on the cheek, and said, "Duty calls. I have an assignment that will take me out of town for about a day or so. I will call you once I assess the situation and determine how long it will take me to complete the job." Amy was half asleep and said, "Okay, call me when you can."

Gregory got into his SUV and raced to get on I-95 to find out what the hell was going on.

He arrived at the Loews in his gray Armani suit, the one with skinny pants and a medium starched shirt. He pulled into the lot to the right of the hotel, reached in the backseat, and pulled out his duffel bag. He gave his keys to the parking attendant; in return he received a parking claim ticket. He entered the hotel from the side door. Parking was horrific in the city.

Gregory called Brendon's cell. "Hey, this is Gregory. I need you to come downstairs and get me access to your room."

Brendon responded casually, "Okay, I will be right down."

He found Brendon dressed in a black Hugo Boss suit, white shirt, no tie, there to greet Gregory at the elevator. Brendon inserted the door key in the slot to the right and hit the PH floor. They rode to the top in silence. As they exited the elevator, Brendon in front leading the way, Gregory studied his swagger. *Why did Emily choose this guy? He is an idiot,* Gregory thought. *I would have taken care of her, but she didn't know I existed back in college. I watched her from afar and even took glimpses of her in the shower without her approval.* Brendon used his key card to gain access to the room and was welcomed by Kyndall's smiling face. "Hi Gregory, I appreciate you being here."

He reached over and gave Kyndall a hug and kiss on the cheek. "Anything for you." After all the pleasantries, it was time to get down to business. Kyndall spoke first. "Brendon, for us to help you, you must tell us what happened."

Gregory listened to the story without judgment. His only question was, "Where is the girl?"

"On the balcony where I left her, earlier this morning."

The group walked to the balcony and Gregory looked. "Were the two of you in the bedroom?"

"Yes," said Brendon. The group moved to the bedroom and looked around.

"When room service came to the room did they see the girl?"

"He didn't see anyone, but knew that I was having dinner with someone."

"How long do you have the room for? One night? Two nights?"

"I have the room for just one night with a late checkout."

"Okay, we have several hours to figure out a plan for getting rid of the body." Gregory took control of the situation. "We need for Emily to be seen with the senator leaving the hotel as a loving couple. Kyndall, maybe you can call her and tell her you need her to prep for an interview with Savannah Guthrie on the *Today Show.*

Savannah wants an exclusive on the community service projects Emily is working on and how she balances her role as wife and mother. The hotel will undergo a shift change at 5:00 p.m., which is the optimal time to get the body out of the hotel. We need to work fast; even though we have seven hours before Brendon must check out, we have less than four hours to get the job done because that is how long it will take Emily to get dressed and drive to DC. Brendon, we need to start cleaning. I brought cleaning supplies with me in the duffle bag." Gregory motioned to the bag on the floor to the right of Brendon. "Start cleaning." As he spoke, he thrust the bag at Brendon while cautioning him, "Brendon, remember, nothing goes in the hotel trash cans. We brought our own industrial bags and will carry the trash with us to burn later."

"Okay." Brendon's whispered reply was as low as his hung head. He reached into the bag to look for the cleaning supplies and cloths. "What's this?"

Gregory halfheartedly turned his head in Brendon's direction, knowing before he saw what he was referring to. "A body bag," he commented without pausing in his work. "Before you start to clean, I need you to put on gloves and clean the body with bleach. Did you use a condom?"

"Of course, I did."

"Did you flush or throw it in the trash?"

"Flushed," said Brendon.

"I want her nails scraped for any traces of DNA left behind. Did she scratch you anywhere?"

"No, I don't have any scratches," Brendon retorted. The third degree was beginning to grow wearisome.

"Where's her cell phone? We need to make sure that it's with her body." Brendon shuffled toward the safe and retrieved the cell phone. "Did she call the burner phone or your personal phone?"

"She called the burner phone," Brendon said with a glowering look toward Gregory.

"Do you have it with you?" Gregory, too, began to grow snappish. Brendon's attitude was trying at the best of times. At a time like this, it made his head hurt. "Where is the burner phone she called?"

Brendon reached in his breast pocket and pulled out a small phone that fit in the palm of his hand.

Gregory grabbed the phone, removed the sim card, and used the heel of his shoe to crush the phone over and over into tiny pieces. With a dustpan and brush pulled from his bag of tricks, he swept the cell phone debris into the dustpan. "Okay, guys, it's on. I'm going downstairs." As he spoke, Gregory grabbed the elevator key from the coffee table and disappeared out of the room, down the hall. Gregory changed his mind and passed the elevator, heading toward the stairs. He stopped on every floor, peeking his head down the hall, looking for a housekeeper. He stopped on several floors before he found someone cleaning on the eighth floor. Gregory darted back into the stairwell and called Kyndall.

"Kyndall, no matter what, don't leave the room."

"Okay," she responded with a puzzled look on her face.

Gregory stepped back onto the eighth floor and casually pulled the fire alarm and rushed toward the housekeeper. "Hey, with the excitement of the fire alarm, I locked myself out of my room. I need to grab my key and briefcase... I have an important meeting and can't be late."

The blaring noise of the fire alarm clouded Joy's judgment, and her eyes impatiently glanced toward the stairs as she heard footsteps descending. "We should exit the building," she yelled over the sound of the alarm.

"Right, I know. I just need to get my briefcase so I can make my meeting. I'm in sales and need to present to a new client, and if I don't land this deal I'll be out of a job." Gregory's eyes left Joy's face and moved toward the floor with a shy smile. Joy didn't want the stranger to lose his job. Reluctantly, she walked up the hall with him and used her universal key to unlock the door at the end of the hall near the stairs; a room Joy had yet to clean.

"Thank you; I appreciate your helping me out. I would be in a bind if I didn't get my briefcase."

"You're welcome." Joy scrambled to the stairs.

Gregory used his back to prop the door open while he pulled latex gloves out of his inside right pocket. The door latch was used to prop the door open as he walked back toward Joy's cart. While everyone used the stairs, Gregory pushed the up arrow on the elevator to the penthouse floor. He exited the elevator, pushed the cart down the hall, and entered Brendon's suite with a swipe of the door key.

Brendon was the first to respond to the housekeeper's cart Gregory was pushing. "What are you going to do with that?"

The ridiculous question Brendon asked received an equally ridiculous response. "I'm changing careers. What in the hell do you think I'm doing with the cart? I need to clean up your mess! Help me dump the body in the cart."

"Why are you so cold? You never used to be this way."

Gregory snapped his neck in the direction of Brendon's voice with high intensity. "Brendon, you are…"

"Okay, you two, cut it out," interrupted Kyndall. "We have too much to do and don't need the infighting."

Brendon picked up Alina's feet and Gregory grabbed her arms. In a swinging motion, Alina landed in the cart with a swish; the contents in the cart cushioned her fall.

"Where are her shoes? We need to find them and put the shoes on her feet." Gregory wiped sweat off his forehead with his handkerchief. Brendon surveyed the room and found Alina's shoes by the coffee table. He brought them over to the cart and handed them to Gregory. Gregory felt devious and refused to take the shoes. "You put them on her feet."

Brendon hesitated for a minute; he was reaching the point

of being uncomfortable with the entire idea. He stared at Alina's motionless body, remembering the fun they'd had hours prior. Brendon took a deep breath to hold back the tears and the hurt in his heart. Gregory snapped his fingers in front of Brendon's face to break his trance-like state. "Put the damn shoes on so we can move the body."

Brendon put Alina's shoes on and stepped back from the body while Kyndall appeared at the bedroom door with the sheets she removed from the bed. They were on a mission not to leave any trace of evidence behind, from the sheets on the bed to the broken glass on the balcony.

Brendon opened the door while Gregory exited the room toward the elevator. He rode to the eighth floor, rolling the cart along the corridor. Gregory found the door he propped open and pushed the cart in the room, closing the door behind him. He picked up the girl from the cart, placed her in the bathtub, and ran cold water. While the water covered Alina's cold, lifeless body, Gregory reached in the cart and grabbed the last remaining items: bleach and the girl's purse. Gregory returned to the bathroom and turned the water off, careful not to let the water overflow onto the floor. He didn't want water to leak to the room below. He took a step back, analyzed the girl in the tub, and turned to the living area where he placed the purse on the bed. Last, he grabbed the bottle of bleach and poured it over the body, careful not to splash the cleaning solution on his expensive suit. "That should do it. If there is any evidence left on the body, sitting in the water with the bleach will contaminate any trace," exclaimed Gregory out loud to no one. Gregory left the bathroom with a satisfied smile playing about his lips. He tossed the empty bleach container in the cart and pushed it out the door. He then peered up the hall and down…still empty. Gregory closed the door behind him and shoved the cart as hard as he could in the original direction he found it. The chatter in the hall moving toward him meant he had no time to transport the cart all the way down the hall. *Ding*, rang the elevator as the doors opened wide. Gregory walked briskly down the hall to descend the stairs to exit the hotel. There was no need for Gregory to go back upstairs…his job was done. He opened the door to the lobby and walked with his head down, avoiding eye contact with anyone. He reached for his cell phone and dialed the familiar number.

"Honey, I'm on my way back home. I will see you soon."

"Drive carefully," replied Amy.

Gregory exited the hotel from a side entrance toward the parking garage. Without a word, he gave the attendant his claim ticket for his car. The valet ran up the steep slope to the parking area while Gregory sat and thought. He would head back to Philadelphia and wait on Kyndall to call him the next time she needed his services. Gregory was convinced there would be a next time. If Brendon was climbing the ladder to the White House, he could bank on Kyndall needing his help sooner rather than later.

Chapter 22

mily pulled up in front of the Loews Madison and gave her keys to the valet. She told him she would be there for a few hours; her husband was meeting the press upstairs in the penthouse suite.

Brendon saw Emily exiting her car from the hotel lobby and rushed to open the door for his beautiful wife.

"Hello, Emily," said Brendon. "You look stunning."

"Thank you."

They two of them embraced and Brendon kissed her on the cheek and whispered, "I love you."

He escorted Emily to the elevator and inserted his key card to gain access to the penthouse suite. They were greeted by Kyndall extending her arms to give Emily a huge hug.

"Hi, Emily, you look beautiful. How are you?"

"I am well. I thought we had an interview with Savannah."

"There was a last-minute scheduling change with the network and the meeting has been pushed back to next week."

"Why didn't you call? I would have turned around."

"I thought it would be a good idea for you and Brendon to spend some quality time together away from all the media attention."

"Perhaps I can check out of the hotel and we can have lunch in the restaurant downstairs."

"I would like that."

"Well, I am going to head back home and let the two of you love birds have some alone time." Kyndall grabbed her purse and keys and headed to the door.

"Oh, Kyndall, don't forget your bag."

"What bag?"

"It looks like an overnight bag. It's not Brendon's so I assumed that it was yours."

Brendon and Kyndall looked at each other like they had something to hide. Oh, but they did. "With the cancelling of the interview I forgot that I brought a change of clothes. You know me, I always have to look my best."

"Do you need some help carrying this downstairs? I can give you a hand."

"Oh, no. This is quite light." Kyndall threw Gregory's duffle bag over her shoulders and bid both Brendon and Emily good-bye.

"I am starved," Brendon exclaimed. "Are you ready for lunch? I have worked up an appetite."

Brendon rolled his suitcase behind him as they walked to the elevator, hand in hand. Once downstairs, Brendon checked out as Emily sat and waited for him. The loud sound of the DC Metro Police alarmed everyone in the hotel and they stared as the police flooded the lobby. The hotel staff escorted them to the eighth floor, where the body had been discovered by the room attendant.

"What's going on?" asked Brendon.

"There was a body found in one of our rooms."

"You don't say. My wife and I were planning to have lunch in the restaurant. Is it safe here?" The manager had overheard the conversation and walked up. "Senator, please have lunch on the hotel for any inconvenience this situation may have caused for you and your wife."

As the senator walked away from the desk, the manager said, "I lived in Pennsylvania prior to moving to DC and voted for you during the last election."

"Thank you so much for your support, Michael." Michael was the name displayed on his name tag. Brendon shook the man's hand.

Brendon went over to where Emily was seated and helped her to her feet. They followed Michael to the restaurant and sat down for lunch.

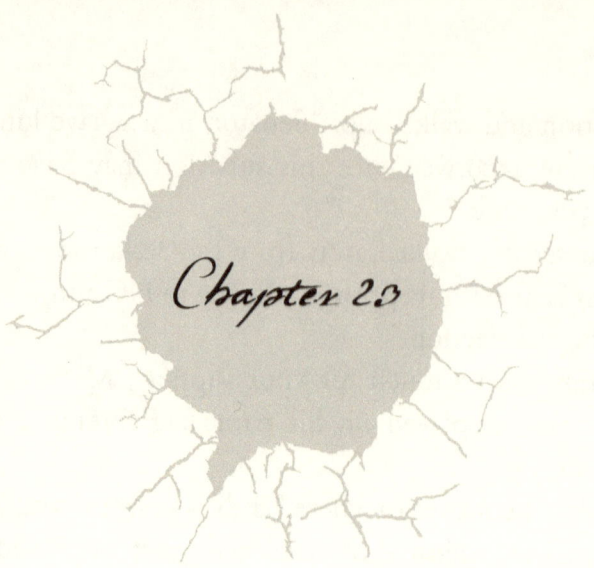

Chapter 23

rendon walks back to the apartment feeling winded from the foot chase down the hall. He sighs as he locks the door behind him. He can't believe that Catherine slipped out and is God knows where in the city. A scary thought crosses his mind: perhaps Catherine went to the police department... but what would she tell? That she had sex for money with a total stranger and was high on booze and heroin? No, she wouldn't go to the police, but she must be found.

Kyndall's chattering on the phone distracts him. Who is she speaking with? It's probably Gregory. She gives him the address and just a little information about what happened, but everything is in code with no names discussed. Within forty minutes, Gregory arrives at the apartment with the tools that he keeps with him always because he never knows when his services will be needed.

Kyndall shares the details of the events up to the time she called him. He listens politely, and tries not to reveal his impatience; there are only two questions that need answering: "How much does the girl know and how did she escape?"

Both Kyndall and Brendon give their versions of the story, but it sounds to Gregory that they were distracted because of the fighting between the two of them; nothing unusual.

As he listens to the details, his mind wanders back to the first time he met Brendon and Kyndall on freshman move-in day.

The door to the dorm was open; Kyndall and Brendon were disagreeing about the classes he should take and who he needed to make friends with because of the family connections she wanted him to have. They were so engrossed in their conversation that they didn't hear Gregory enter the room behind them. He didn't have many possessions, just two suitcases and his olive-green duffle bag. "Hi, I'm Gregory." As he extended his right hand, the duffle bag fell to the crease of his arm. Kyndall scornfully examined Gregory from the top of his head to the black Converse on his feet.

Brendon gave his mother a smug look, reached over her, and shook Gregory's hand. "Hi Gregory, I'm Brendon and this is my mother, Kyndall."

Kyndall turned with an annoyed sigh. "It's nice to meet you, Gregory," spilled out of her mouth, all in one breath.

Brendon turned his attention toward Gregory, dismissing Kyndall's pouty frown. "Do you need help unpacking? Where's the rest of your stuff?"

"No, I am good. I don't need any help. I don't have much to unpack."

Kyndall's stare was dark as she eyed Gregory. What was his story? Why didn't he have much luggage? Soon, her smile turned soft as she realized that Gregory would be useful to her. He came from meager beginnings, which she could use to her benefit when she needed a "special favor."

Zoe shuddered at what she saw in her rearview mirror. After he picked up the last duffle bag from the truck, she sped off down the street with only a glance in the rearview mirror. "That bastard, he killed Tara, my older sister. I know he did it." Zoe pounded the steering wheel with both hands and screamed. "The homicide detective claimed that there wasn't enough solid evidence against him, so he was never charged, just a person of interest in the case." Zoe was a good Christian woman who promised her sister she would care for her son until he was eighteen. She felt as though she owed it to Tara that her only son had the best education, so she encouraged him to apply to Temple University, where he received a full academic scholarship; the news was exciting because she was done with that monster. Gregory was waving to her with a cryptic smile that made chills run throughout her body. The highway exit could not come up fast enough. Once she was sure she was safe, Zoe picked up her phone and found Ruth's number. She proceeded to dial with urgency.

"Hello, Ruth, this is Zoe again."

"Oh, hi, Zoe."

"I want to put my house on the market. I need to get out of town as quickly as possible. Can we start the paperwork tonight?"

"Sure. I can come over with the paperwork for you to sign later today."

"Perfect. I will see you then." Zoe needed to get as far away from Gregory as she could.

Chapter 24

*G*regory asks both Kyndall and Brendon a second time, "What all does she know?"

"Brendon, you can give Gregory the details of what happened prior to your calling me. How did you meet the girl?"

"I didn't do anything differently this time. I followed my same routine. I called Stella's private number and told her I wanted to see Brandy, but she informed me that Brandy was unavailable. She asked me if I wanted another girl and I told her I did."

"Wait a minute, let me get this straight. You used a different escort and you didn't think that was something I needed to know? How could you be so stupid? We don't know her, nor do we know what she's capable of doing. I had vetted Brandy and I could trust her."

"Mother, I needed the company, that was all."

Kyndall rolls her eyes at Brendon in disgust. "I swear, sometimes I don't think you want to be married or want the White House."

"Mother, how can you say that? You know I love Emily and can't bear to lose her. I don't know what I would do without her."

"You need to start acting like you want to save your marriage. Emily is getting frustrated with you, and I am losing my patience with you as well." Kyndall flops on the sofa, shaking her head at the thought of Brendon's reckless behavior.

Brendon turns his attention from his mother and pleads his case to Gregory instead. "I have been working under Stella's discretion for years. I felt safe with her recommendation on a different girl."

Stella Thaxton provided an upscale escort service and took new clients by invitation only. She came highly recommended from several of his poker buddies who sat on the bench. It was Stella's idea to give Brendon the alias just in case her private records got in the hands of the wrong person. If anyone subpoenaed her client book, they would only find the alias "Andy." To make matters more secure, Brendon has leverage over Stella...

Gregory's voice brings Brendon's attention back to his current crisis. "How did the girl know where to meet you?"

"Stella asked me if I would be in the usual location."

"Which is here, the apartment?"

"Yes, the apartment is the only address Stella has. She texted it to Catherine; nothing out of the ordinary."

"Brendon, I would have to agree with your mother. Using an escort other than Brandy is alarming because we don't know this Catherine girl and she can't be trusted. I have a feeling that *Catherine*," Gregory motions air quotes, "is a wild card. I would have never approved of the switch. I need to find this girl and I need to find her fast. Give me your phone."

Brendon's sharp stare cut through Gregory like a knife. He thrust his phone into Gregory's chest. Gregory catches it with his right hand and extends his arm towards Brendon. "Unlock the phone."

"You're the professional hacker, you unlock it." Brendon is aware just how much he sounds like a peevish child. He tries not to blush.

"Don't get smug with me. Unlock the damn phone!"

Brendon snatches the phone from Gregory and enters his code.

Kyndall intervenes, "Brendon, I know you're upset; don't take it out on Gregory. He is only here to help."

"I know. Sorry, man."

"No problem. We are all under pressure right now."

Brendon hands the unlocked phone back to Gregory, who peruses the photos that were sent to Emily. Gregory examines the photos silently, not judging, just assessing the situation. It takes him minutes to identify the number from which the pictures were sent. He taps the display screen; everyone in the room jumps when the phone rings. They look around the room for the phone. "The safe!" exclaims Brendon while running in the bedroom closet to retrieve the phone. There is no need to be coy with Gregory at this point. When he enters the living room Brendon immediately hands the phone to him. "Thanks." Gregory picks up his briefcase from the floor and places it on the kitchen island. He then connects Catherine's phone to one of the two lap tops. It is magical watching Gregory work; his craft, the movement and rhythm, is effortless.

"Ah, got it. I am in her phone."

"That is great," Kyndall blurts. For a second, Brendon and Gregory stop what they are doing and look towards her; they had forgot she was in the room because she had been so quiet.

Gregory's attention is back to Catherine's phone. He snoops around the phone for what seem like hours but is only ten minutes. He can find some interesting information on Catherine through her social media accounts and photos. Gregory pauses at a touching photo of Catherine's mother undergoing chemotherapy. Catherine is holding her frail mother's hand as the liquid penetrates her mother's veins. The caption reads, "Mom and I will beat cancer, cancer won't beat us." Gregory downloads the photo to his laptop and proceeds to download a photo of Catherine to the Pennsylvania and New York Department of Motor Vehicles to find an address for her.

"Okay, our unidentified girl is Catherine Wilson. She has a driver's license from the state of Pennsylvania. From the state of New York, she only has an ID card. Catherine used a ride share service from the address on the Pennsylvania driver's license."

"Do you think that's where she lives?" asks Kyndall.

"No, I think she lives in New York now and the address on her driver's license is her parents' home. I do have a hunch that she is still in the city for now."

Anxiously Brendon asks, "What do we do now?"

Gregory contemplates the question as he twirls the pen he is holding. A few moments go by and Gregory stays within his character. He goes into cleanup mode. "Brendon, I need you and Kyndall to clean up the apartment and make it look like new; clean everything, everywhere, and don't forget to take the trash out when you leave. In the morning, call a professional cleaning service to clean the apartment; then call a moving company to move the furniture and donate it to Goodwill. Who orchestrated the lease deal for the apartment?"

Kyndall pipes up. "I did."

"I know you are careful, but I have to ask. Whose name is the lease in?"

"I used a fake corporation to establish the lease; because I paid six months in advance, no one asked questions."

"Okay, call the licensing company, break the lease, and pay whatever fees. Don't meet with them in person. We don't need anyone describing how you look to the authorities if it comes down to that." Gregory works in silence, closing everything down. "Have you used the fake corporation name for anything else?"

Brendon and Kyndall think back and reply simultaneously, "No."

"Good."

Gregory walks to the door with briefcase in hand. He turns to the group. "I'm going to follow the lead to the address in Philly. I will let you know what I find."

*C*atherine runs down the hall like her life depends on it, because, simply put, it does. She picks up the pace by pumping her legs higher and channeling her mental energy on the finish line, just as she did running cross country in high school. It appears it was a decade ago that she was in high school receiving the scholarship for running, but it was just four years ago. Catherine dropped out of high school in her junior year to care for her mother, who was diagnosed with cancer. The bills were piling up and her mother didn't need the worry of warding off bill collectors while she was in the fight for her life.

Each day Catherine came home from school to find her mother weeping because she hurt all over. The doctor said that the ovarian cancer had spread to her bones and gave her months to live. Catherine was devastated when she heard the news of her mother's diagnosis and the short time she would have her mother on earth. Her mother would miss all her firsts: serious relationship, marriage, wedding, and baby. She struggled with the news because her mother was the one person in the world who cared

"What about the city surveillance cameras?"

"Destroyed. The only loose ends we have are the two detectives. I will pay them a visit and send a strong message to back off."

"Okay, I trust your judgment. Let me know when you are done."

"By the way, you need to check your boyfriend Dennis; I don't do well with threats."

"Okay, I will have a conversation with him. I am sure he didn't mean any harm."

"Yeah, right."

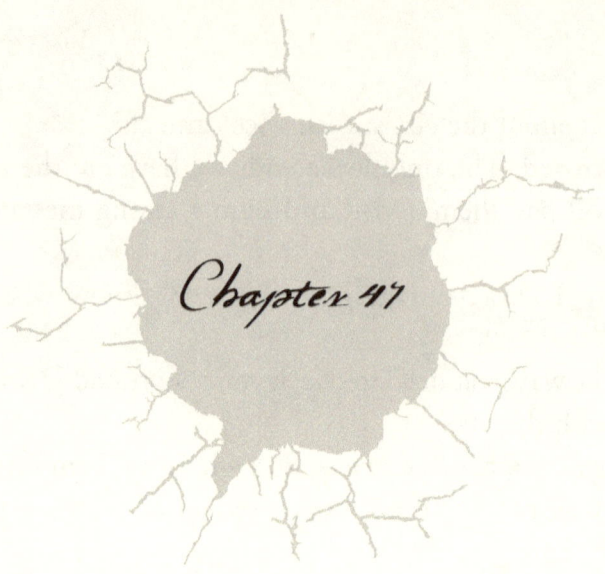

Chapter 47

Oliver and Dakota pulled up in front of Alina's apartment building. Oliver showed the young man at the concierge desk his badge and introduced himself and Dakota as homicide detectives.

"Do you have a moment for a few questions?"

"Yes."

"Do you know this lady?" Detective Hall pulled out his iPhone, which displayed Alina's photo.

Kenneth took a second glance and he recognized Alina. He'd had a secret crush on her from the moment he laid eyes on her. He knew she was out of his league with her fancy clothes; she looked so well taken care of and he didn't have the means to give her what she was used to. He lived off the salary of a concierge for an apartment building. It wasn't bad but he had to work a second job to make ends meet. Kenneth never bothered to ask her out. He didn't think she knew his name.

"I know her. Why is a homicide detective looking for her? Is she okay?"

"No, Kenneth, she is dead."

Kenneth was crushed; the woman who danced around in his dreams was gone. "Oh, no." Kenneth stumbled backward and Oliver reached to steady him.

"When was the last time you saw Alina Ivanovich?"

"I saw her last evening. She was dressed up, so I assumed she was going out on a date. The car service was outside to pick her up."

"Do you recall the name of the service?"

"City Limousine. She uses the service every time she goes out on a date."

"Can you let us in her apartment?"

"Sure."

Kenneth used his key card and entered it into the slot. He pressed the button for the fifth floor, tears welling up in the corners of his eyes.

The detectives were staring at Kenneth's back, which shielded them from seeing the lone tear fall from his burning eyes. Kenneth pressed his index finger and thumb of his right hand to soak up the remaining tears. The beep of the elevator alerted him that they had reached Alina's floor. Everyone exited in silence while following Kenneth to the first apartment on the right. He used the fob on his key ring to unlock the door. The three of them stepped into the apartment. Kenneth took in Alina's immaculate apartment and a deep breath and he smelled her signature scent. He would miss her dearly.

Oliver turned to Kenneth. "Thank you."

"You are welcome."

Oliver thought that Kenneth would take the cue and leave. When he didn't, Oliver shot Dakota a look and shook his head in amazement. Dakota turned to Kenneth and spoke gently. "Kenneth, thank you for your help. Detective Hall and I will look and close the door behind us."

"Oh, okay." Kenneth turned and exited the apartment.

The two detectives moved from room to room, looking in her journal, at her prescriptions, and in all her drawers. There wasn't any place in the apartment that was sacred to the detectives. They were especially eager to find her cell phone, but nothing turned up. Oliver took a step back and viewed the room from the vantage point of the door as one would first enter the apartment. He moved to the doorway of each room and quickly scanned.

Oliver frowned. "What's missing?"

"Besides her phone, I don't see anything else that I would think is missing."

"Do you think it's strange that there's not a computer—a desktop, laptop, or tablet?"

Dakota scanned the room and didn't find one either. "What person doesn't have some type of electronic device?" They were both thinking when Oliver got a phone call.

Isabel's school was on the phone, alerting him that Isabel needed to be picked up. They had tried to call Bridgette, his wife, but did not receive an answer. Odd, Oliver thought. He told the school that he would be over right away to pick up Isabel. Then Oliver called and called Bridgette. When each call went to voice mail, his heart started to beat uncontrollably. His detective instinct told him that something was wrong.

"Oliver, is everything okay?"

"No, Bridgette hasn't picked up Isabel from daycare and it is after six. I just tried to call her and the phone goes directly to voice mail."

"What do you need me to do?"

"Will you go by the house and check on Bridgette? I will pick up Isabel. We can meet up at my house."

"Oliver, you take the car and I will take an Uber to your house."

Oliver sped toward the daycare to pick up Isabel. The sinking feeling in his stomach convinced him that his instincts were correct.

Dakota approached the house. Everything looked normal from the outside. She paid for her fare and gave the Uber driver an extra tip for getting her there as quickly as possible.

Dakota approached the front door and knocked loud and hard. "Bridgette!"

It seemed odd that there weren't any lights on inside or outside the house. The days were shorter and it got darker earlier. Dakota knocked on the door several more times without an answer. She rang the doorbell repeatedly. She didn't hear footsteps inside the house so she reached for the spare key on the upper right ledge of the door frame.

She stepped inside. "Bridgette!" The house was pitch black, so Dakota groped along the wall to the front entrance for a light switch. Her head began to swim as she was overwhelmed with a stench she couldn't place right away. It merely heightened her anxiety. "Bridgette, Bridgette, it's me, Dakota!"

The smell is rotten eggs!

Recognition dawned on her too late… When Dakota turned the light switch on, the entire house erupted in flames. The natural gas leak had been sparked when the light switch was turned on. Dakota managed to stumble from the living room to the front yard with burns over half of her body. She screamed and screamed at the pain of her clothes stuck to her body like a second skin. Neighbors in each direction flooded their yards, jamming the phone lines to 911. Oliver heard the scanner calls to his home and raced home with Isabel blissfully asleep in the backseat.

Oliver arrived at the scene and started to weep as he took in the sight of the EMTs working on Dakota, loading her into the back of the ambulance to take her to MedStar Washington Hospital's Burn Center.

The firefighters were feeding the house water to put out the flames.

Morgan, the fire chief, approached Oliver when he pulled up in front of the house.

"What happened?"

"There was an explosion. It looks as though it was a natural gas leak, but I need to complete a full investigation and give a formal report. Don't quote me on my comment. I still have work to do at the scene."

"I am looking for my wife. Was she in the house?"

"There is another body, but the medical examiner must determine the cause of death and gender of the deceased." Morgan added, "Speak of the devil," when Punky arrived on the scene. She moved toward Oliver and the firefighter. The chief walked off as Oliver turned to find himself nose to nose with Punky. Thank god. They both embraced.

"Oliver, I am so sorry to hear what happened to Dakota. Where is Bridgette?"

"I'm not sure. I think she was in the house when it went up in flames. Morgan did find a charred body."

"Where is Isabel?"

"She is asleep in the car."

Punky ran to the car and opened the door to the backseat to find Isabel asleep. With a drawn-out sigh, she unbuckled the car seat and laid Isabel's head on her shoulder, carrying her to her father.

The chief of police approached Oliver. "I heard the accident over the scanner. Where is Dakota?"

"She was burned when the house exploded."

"Where is Bridgette?"

"Morgan found a charred body in the house and thinks that it's Bridgette, but we can't know for sure."

"Oliver, there isn't anything you can do tonight. We need to find you a place to stay tonight. You can stay with me for as long as you need. Isabel needs a stable place to stay. The spare key is where we used to keep it."

"I can't."

"You need to think about the well-being of your daughter."

Oliver smiled. "Thank you." He knew that Punky was right and made sense. Reluctantly, he took Isabel, who was still asleep though all the commotion, back to the car.

Punky waved as they backed out of the driveway, heading in the direction of her house.

She walked toward Morgan. "Where's the body?"

"Follow me."

Punky and Morgan walked through the rubble in the house. Punky was thorough and wanted to see the body where it was found.

"My preliminary finding is a natural gas leak. The gas line was tampered with and when the gas came in contact with the open flame, possibly a pilot light, that added the element for the explosion. DC Natural Gas was on the scene cutting off the gas line to houses on the block."

Dakota was flown to the burn center, but went into shock. She never made it through the night.

Chapter 48

unky completed the final medical examiner's report that noted the female deceased at the crime scene was the wife of Oliver Hall, but she had a gunshot wound to the leg and chest. Morgan, the fire chief, had indicated that the gas line was cut. Both Bridgette and Dakota's deaths were classified as homicides.

Punky felt her body go cold. How could she help Oliver move past these murders?

On the other side of town, a very different conversation had taken place. Gregory called Kyndall.

"The message has been sent."

He said nothing more and hung up the phone.

"Ms. McCormick, can you hear me?"

Reese opened her eyes and looked around the unrecognizable room. She couldn't make out where she was but saw the light flashing in her eyes. She blinked.

"We are glad you're awake. You have been asleep for days. How do you feel?"

Reese moved her head slightly to the right toward the voice speaking to her.

"Where am I?"

"Honey, you're in the hospital. We were all worried about you."

Reese reached out to touch her aching head. She felt the scratchy cotton feel of bandages.

"My head hurts."

"You can manage your pain by pressing this button. That will give you a dose of morphine."

Reese picked up the drip and found her hands were bandaged as well. She pressed the drip and felt the warm sensation of medicine flowing through her body. Limb by limb, she started to relax. She had to concentrate to even move her leg half an inch. Her relaxed muscles and mind put her back into a deep sleep. Reese's dreams took her to a place where she was in a kitchen cooking dinner. There was a baby in a high chair and laughter throughout the house. A man came in the front door and gave her a passionate kiss, with a bouquet of flowers.

"Hello, honey. How was your day?"

Reese kissed him again. She was the happiest she had ever been, with a smile that could light the pathway for ships to make it ashore safely in the dead of night.

"Reese, this is Dr. Thompson. Can you hear me?"

Reese could hear someone calling her name, but refused to emerge from her happy place. She realized that this could be the future she'd always wanted.

"Reese, can you hear me?"

The doctor used his index finger and thumb to open her eyes and shine the flashlight at her pupils.

Reese released the dream, but knew that this was where she wanted to be when she left the hospital. She would search for happiness and she knew it was out there waiting for her.

"Reese, you have sustained a head injury and cuts to both your wrists. We bandaged them because you were picking at the stitches. We take the bandages off during the day so that the wounds can get some air and heal. We are going to take the bandages off now. Will you promise not to pick at them?"

"Okay."

Dr. Thompson began removing the bandages. "Do you have any questions about your injuries?"

"No. How long will I be in the hospital?"

"Later today we will do a CT scan to ensure there isn't any brain swelling. If there isn't, then you will be released tomorrow. Is there anyone at home who can help you for a few days until you are able to get up and around?"

"I don't have anyone I can stay with. I live alone."

"We won't be able to release you until you find someone to take you home."

"Okay, I am sure I can find someone."

"I will make my rounds in the morning. If you need anything let the nurses at the station know. I want you to stay in bed for a couple of days, until you can build up your strength."

"Thanks."

Reese looked at the wounds on her wrists and remembered everything that happened the night of the crash. She knew that Doris had tried to kill her, but she couldn't be mad at her. She forgave Doris because she had destroyed Doris' marriage. *If I channel negative energy toward Doris, I will never get the family that I saw in my dreams. I no longer want to cause harm to others.*

Suddenly, the prayer she prayed when she was stuck on the side of the cliff floated through her mind.

"Heavenly Father, I want to live. Please send someone to rescue me. If you see fit to answer this prayer I will live a life you will be proud of and I can face myself in the mirror again. I have made mistakes in the past but now is the time to prove that I can be a better person."

Reese picked up the phone and called Ally, a waitress who worked at the Watering Hole, part-time.

"Reese, it's so good to hear from you. We were all so worried about you. Are you okay?"

"I am getting there."

"What happened?"

"I…I don't remember. The doctor says that my accident was so traumatic, I blocked out everything that happened to me that night."

"You poor thing."

"Ally, I was wondering if you could pick me up from the hospital tomorrow. The doctor said that if my CT scan comes back normal, I can go home."

"Oh sure, I'm off from both the Watering Hole and Pinnacle Home Healthcare. I don't have a sitting job tomorrow."

"Okay. I will give you a call tomorrow. I appreciate this. You are my only family here."

"No problem. I will see you tomorrow."

The shadow at the door moved down the hall and used the far exit stairs to the right and left the hospital.

He pulled out his phone and called his foe. "Why did Emily's mother try to kill her husband's girlfriend?"

"What? What are you talking about?"

"I am investigating Doris Massey, Emily's mother. She tried to kill Reese, her husband's girlfriend. I am going to close the case, citing I do not have enough evidence on her, but she killed her husband and by the grace of God, Reese did not die in the accident. What do you have down there, a family of murderers? I suspect that family is keeping you busy."

Gregory thought about what Dennis said, and he agreed, but would never give him the satisfaction of being right. "Are you sure it was Doris who killed her husband and attempted to murder the girlfriend?"

"Don't question me! I am good at what I do. And yes, that's where my investigation has led me."

Gregory had to agree that Dennis was an excellent detective; that's why Kyndall recruited him to be on her team. Dennis was underpaid and Kyndall exploited him to get what she wanted. Gregory almost felt sorry for him, if he had feelings toward Dennis, which he didn't. "What's the girl's name? I will handle it."

"Oh, you are doing a fabulous job handling the events thus far. Let's see, there are detectives questioning me about Emily and Brendon, and now the rogue mother, Doris, trying to kill her husband's girlfriend, Reese, and successfully murdering her husband, Steve. You keep handling Kyndall's 'investments' carelessly, and you will find yourself either dead or…dead. You know too much for her to keep you alive. I will be happy to move up in the organization when you are dead."

"You smug bastard. You think she will choose you over me?"

"Yes, I do and you know it."

Gregory took a moment to reflect on what his adversary was saying. He knew that he was only a pawn in Kyndall's overall plan for Brendon to be President. He cleared his throat to break the silence. "I will take care of it."

"You say that every time, and I have to clean up your mess." Dennis ended the call without another word, leaving Gregory to doubt his position in Kyndall's master plan.

Chapter 49

*C*atherine had always had an exciting life, and Sheila was thrilled to be a part of the excitement now.

"Okay, what you need me to do?"

"Let me get dressed and we can work out a plan."

Sheila and Catherine walked back to Catherine's mother's house, laughing and talking about good times. Before Catherine veers off down the back alley they embrace. "Call me soon," yelled Sheila. Catherine climbed the fire escape and opened the window to her mother's bedroom, where she found her sleeping peacefully. She walked, careful not to wake her mother, to her childhood bedroom to start packing. She flipped the left corner of the mattress and pulled out $500 cash and stashed it in her purse. She had purchased a ticket with her credit card for the Megabus that would leave within the hour from 30th Street Station to NYC. She took a second look at herself in the mirror and decided to disguise her look by pinning her hair up and putting on a brunette wig that she used to wear in high school for fun. She stopped by the kitchen for some snacks for the long ride. Catherine entered her mother's room and gave her a kiss on the cheek and left her a letter. She crossed her overnight bag over her body and left through the window, the same way she entered.

Catherine trotted two blocks down the street and hailed a taxi to the Megabus stop.

Sheila ignored it when the door to a black SUV opened and closed, and the driver picked up his pace and yelled, "Excuse me, excuse me!"

She turned around to hear the voice of a stranger.

"Hey, I was wondering if you saw my lost puppy?"

"No, I haven't seen a puppy."

Gregory grabbed Sheila by the throat and asked, "Are you Catherine?"

Shelia tried to respond but nothing came out except a choking gurgle.

"You heard me. Are you Catherine? I will snap your neck if you don't answer my question."

Shelia no longer thought this was fun or even a game. The heat of the man's breath on her neck was frightening. She was afraid that this man would kill her if she didn't tell him what he wanted.

"Do you know where Catherine is? I won't hurt you if you tell me where she is. I will let you go."

"She wasn't sure if someone was after her, so she asked me to act as though I was her to serve as a distraction so she could go upstairs and get her stuff."

"Who's upstairs?"

"Her mother, Nancy; she's dying of cancer. Catherine couldn't leave town without saying good-bye to her."

"Leave town? She doesn't live here?"

"No, she lives in New York City."

"Why was she in Philly?"

"She needed to earn extra money to afford a home health-care sitter for her mother."

The driver loosened his grip on Shelia's neck.

"Catherine said she didn't mean to take the pictures of Andy. She's sorry, so you can stop looking for her."

"Did she tell you anything about Andy?"

"No, but she thought he was an influential person."

"How influential?"

"She wasn't sure."

"Do you know who he is?"

"No, I wasn't there but she described him to me as I sketched his facial features. After I reviewed the drawing, he didn't seem like anyone I knew either."

"Where is she going?"

"Back to NYC. Can I go now? I told you what you wanted."

"Oh, yeah. I am sorry about the confusion." Gregory extended his hand as a peace offering to Sheila. She eagerly reached for his hand, but Gregory had other plans. Mechanically, he reached for Sheila's head and with a sharp twist, he snapped her neck. Sheila's limp body fell in the middle of the street, but Gregory took no notice. He jogged back to his car and took off his gloves before getting back in the black SUV. He sped down the street, racing to the bus stop to find Catherine. The thump was satisfying as he ran over the girl's dead body. It rivaled the image of her lying cold in the street with tire tracks across her face.

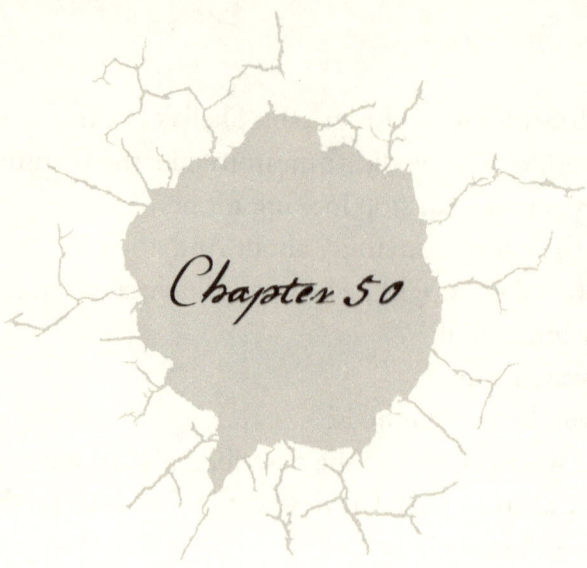

Chapter 50

Catherine crossed her arms and shivered her leg impatiently as she waited for the bus to arrive. It was taking too long and she was far too conspicuous in the thin crowd. She studied each face, wondering if someone was chasing her. Catherine had always been street smart and knew to trust her gut. She looked up the street and saw the blue bus with the larger-than-life man on the side. What a sight for sore eyes. The bus pulled over and the driver got off. He was speaking with the local agent as there were fifteen more minutes before passengers could board. Catherine was the second person in line and was glad when the crowd started to thicken. She hoped it would shield her from whoever was following her.

The fifteen minutes seemed like an eternity. Catherine boarded the bus and took a seat at the back, next to the window; she loved the window seat so she could people watch while everyone else boarded.

Gregory pulled up and asked the driver if he could board the bus because he was looking for his sister to say good-bye.

"Only ticketed passengers can board the bus. Do you have a ticket?"

"No, like I said my sister is on the bus and left before I had the opportunity to say good-bye."

"You can't board the bus."

"How much is a ticket?"

"This bus is sold out."

"Sell me a ticket so I can say good-bye to my sister. Here is a hundred-dollar bill plus the cost of the ticket."

"It would be unethical to sell you a seat on the bus when no seats are available."

Gregory moved to the left, trying to enter the bus, and the driver moved to the left. Gregory darted to the right, and the driver darted to the right.

"Look, man, I don't want any trouble. You can't enter the bus." The driver shouted to another agent, "We have a problem. Call the police!"

"I don't want any trouble."

"Me either," said the driver, "so back off."

Gregory raised his hands with his palms out. "Okay."

Catherine watched the man at the door trying to get in and thought he could be the guy who was after her. She sank lower in her seat.

The other agent asked Gregory to back away from the bus as they needed to prepare to leave. Gregory complied and watched as the bus pulled away from the curb.

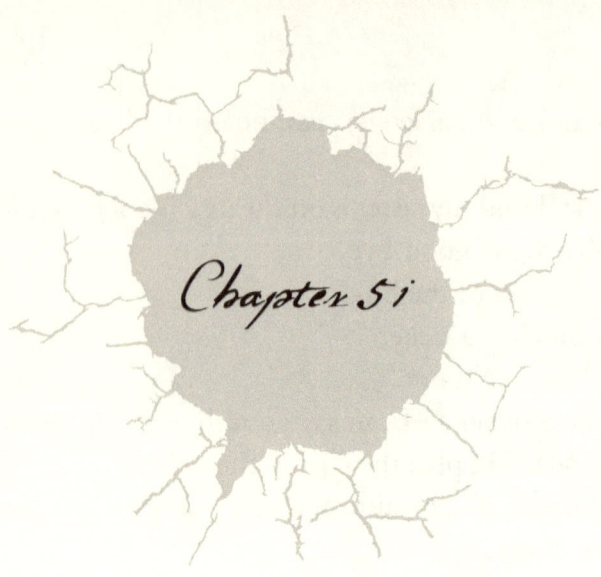

$\mathcal{G}$regory got back into his car and headed to Catherine's mother's house. He parked about a block away because of the police barricade. He walked the sidewalk, careful not to look as though he was interested in the crime in the street. He knocked on the door to the row home and a fragile lady opened the door.

"Can I help you?"

"Hi. Catherine is a friend of my son and she left this morning and he wasn't able to say good-bye. Is it possible for you to give her his number? He is so smitten with her that I wanted to try to reach her for him. I would think a call from her would brighten his day."

Nancy smiled. She knew her daughter was a looker and remembered how it was when she was younger. She was sure the way this gentleman's son was feeling was the same way she had felt about Catherine's father.

"Yes, I will make sure she gets the number. Apparently, she left in the middle of the night and didn't want to wake me. Thank you so much. Have a nice day."

"You too."

"By the way, what is your son's name?"

Gregory paused. "I am sorry for my manners; his name is Andy. My name is Gregory."

"It's nice to meet you, Gregory. My name is Nancy."

"It's my pleasure. Have a nice day."

Gregory walked off with a smile. At least he had more information about Catherine than he had hours ago. So, he just needed to wait for her to call.

Chapter 52

"Ally, this is Reese. My CT scan came back normal and the doctor is releasing me from the hospital after he gives me one final examination. Can you pick me up?"

"Yes, I can be there within the hour. Is that okay?"

"Perfect. I will see you soon."

Just then, Dr. Thompson walked in and asked how she was. "I'm feeling great, Doctor. I can't wait to go home," Reese said.

"I reviewed all your test results and you are ready to be released. You will be on bed rest today and tomorrow and can go back to work on Thursday. Very light duty. Do you need a doctor's note?"

"Yeah, I'm thinking about changing careers. I haven't had the best of luck waiting tables."

Ally was a sight for sore eyes when she entered the room, "Hey, Reese."

"Thank you so much for agreeing to take me home."

"No problem."

"If you changed careers what would you do?"

"Reese, are you looking to leave the Watering Hole?"

"I am. I want a career where I can have a normal life and meet someone I can start a family with. This accident was a warning sign that I need to get my life together." Reese started to cry.

"Oh, Reese, don't cry. I can get you on at Pinnacle Healthcare. You can start out sitting with patients and then I can help you study for your CNA license."

"Are there any openings?"

"We always have something available," said Ally. "When we go back to my apartment I can call."

"See? All things work out," said Dr. Thompson.

The hospital transporter rolled the wheelchair into the room. Reese was helped into the wheelchair with Ally following close behind.

"Do you have everything?"

Reese took a second look around the room and tears formed in her eyes. She had been in the hospital for days' and didn't have one flower or card from a friend or a loved one. No one cared whether she was dead or alive. It renewed her determination to change her path.

The transporter took Reese downstairs where Ally pulled the car around and helped with loading Reese into the car.

Chapter 53

Ally drove Reese to her apartment and helped her to her bedroom. Ally took the sofa. Reese buried her body in between the sheets and fell into a deep sleep.

Ally knew how it felt not to have someone to depend on, so she made herself available to her friends and family when they were in need. Reese certainly needed a friend right then.

Ally picked up her home phone and dialed the number to work. "Sabrina, hey, this is Ally. I have a friend who is getting back on her feet and needs a job. She is smart and bright just like me. Do we have a sitting job for her? She is interested in getting her CNA license later."

"How soon can she start?"

"She just got out of the hospital and can start in three days."

"This is perfect because we have a sitting job for a woman who has ovarian cancer and needs someone to make sure that she takes her medication, gets three meals a day, and goes to her doctor's appointments. Do you think that your friend would be interested?"

"Yes, this is perfect. By the way, her name is Reese. If you can send over her new hire paperwork to my email, I will ensure she fills it out and I can drop it off when I come to work tomorrow."

"Sounds like a plan. I will give you the address tomorrow as well."

"Great. Thank you so much."

"I can always use reliable help."

Chapter 54

*R*eese followed the doctor's orders and rested for three days at Ally's house, binge watching her favorite shows on Netflix. She was looking forward to starting work at Pinnacle Healthcare as a sitter. Ally's boss had told her if she did a good job with this assignment there would be other opportunities to do more with the company. She was just thankful that someone had given her a chance and she could leave the Watering Hole. Before Reese left for her assignment, she opened her email and read the background on the patient so she was familiar with their needs. Nancy was the name of her patient. She was currently undergoing chemotherapy for ovarian cancer.

Reese turned off the computer and finished dressing for work in her purple scrubs and black clogs. She hailed a taxi and gave him the address to Nancy's home. She arrived ten minutes before the start of her shift.

"Excuse me, miss, excuse me?"

Reese stopped and turned around. The heavy pipe iron came across her head with a hard blow. She fell to the ground and the assailant hit her multiple times, over and over, until she no longer moved her arms or legs.

Gregory picked up the body and placed it in the back of the SUV. He crossed the street to where Reese was headed and rang the doorbell.

It took Nancy several minutes to come to the door, dressed and ready to go to her chemotherapy treatment. "Oh, hello. I was expecting Reese from Pinnacle Healthcare."

"Yes, ma'am. Reese couldn't make it today; she wasn't feeling well and the service sent me. When I found out that I would be working with you, I jumped at the opportunity because of our connection with Catherine. Isn't this a coincidence?"

"Well, this is a nice surprise. Are you ready to go?"

"I am; I didn't quite get the information where we are going this morning because of the change in sitters."

"That is no problem. We are going to the hospital for my chemotherapy treatment. Let me get my purse." Nancy walked back into the tiny home and retrieved her purse, keys, and a blanket from the table in the hall. She reappeared and locked the door behind her.

"Shall we?" Gregory extended his arm to Nancy.

Nancy smiled and looped her arm with Gregory's. He led her to the SUV, smiling at the thought of Reese's body growing colder in the trunk.

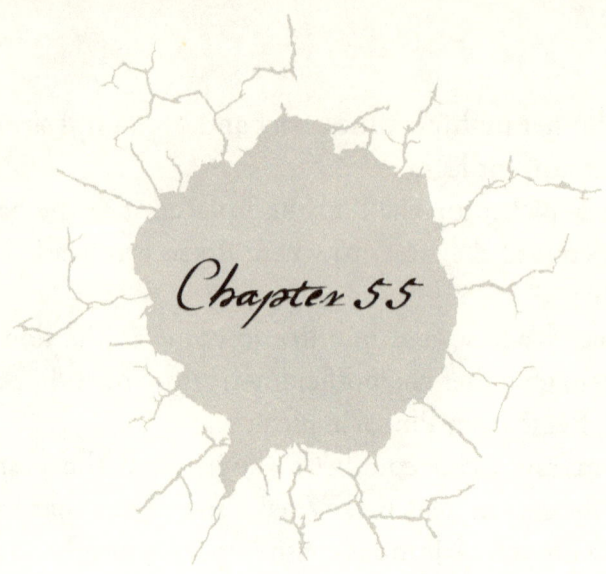

Chapter 55

Gregory pulled up in front of the hospital and got out, opening the passenger side door for Nancy. He ran in through the double doors and got her a wheelchair so she didn't have to walk.

"Nancy, are you comfortable?"

"You are so caring. Yes, I am good. It's nice to have such a handsome man fussing over me."

"It takes little effort when I have a beautiful woman on my arm."

Nancy blushed a little and patted Gregory on the hand.

The two of them meandered down the hall to the reception area where he checked her in. The nurse immediately called Nancy back. "Gregory, if there is something you need to do, you can leave. My infusion treatment lasts for two hours."

"Oh, no. The only place I want to be is here with you. I will wait out in the lobby. Take your blanket so you are not too cold during your treatment."

"You are so kind, Gregory."

Gregory stood at the door and waited until Nancy was out of sight. He calmly walked back to the lobby and straight out the door. He hopped into his SUV parked on the curb and sped off to bury the dead body. A good thing too. Even though the days were getting cooler, the heat from the sun was causing his truck to smell like a dead corpse.

Chapter 58

This was an unplanned kill, so Gregory didn't have any of his supplies in his car. He pulled up into his neighborhood, opened the garage door, and pulled the car in before closing the door. Once certain he was alone, Gregory quickly gathered a few supplies and placed them on top of Reese's body. He backed out of the driveway, but realized he didn't have enough time to drive out of the state to dump the body. He had to get back to the hospital to pick up Nancy and couldn't be late. He drove to the outskirts of the city to a deserted wooded area, opened the trunk, and removed the digging tools. He picked up the body with his gloved hands and tossed her in the woods. Before doing so, Gregory checked his watch. He must hurry; he had only thirty minutes to get back to the hospital to pick up Nancy.

Chapter 57

*G*regory arrived at the hospital and ran through the lobby, sweaty and hot. He reached the lobby desk. "Is Nancy ready?"

"She just finished up. She went to the ladies' room."

Gregory took a tissue from the receptionist desk and wiped his face.

"Gregory, I'm ready."

"How was your treatment?"

"I am tired. Speaking of looking tired, are you okay? You look flushed."

"Yeah, I had a breakfast burrito that didn't agree with me."

"You shouldn't eat all of that unhealthy food. You young people eat fast food that has all those additives. God knows where they come from."

"Yes, ma'am. I will watch what I eat."

"Good."

"Your chariot awaits."

Chapter 58

*B*y the time Gregory arrived at Nancy's home, she was
fast asleep. He reached into her purse and grabbed
her house keys as he didn't want to disturb her. He picked her up
and carried her to the door. He unlocked the door and kicked it
closed behind him. Once securely inside, he carried her upstairs
to her bedroom and covered her with the blanket on the foot
of the bed. Gregory used this as an opportunity to walk across
the hall and search Catherine's room. He wasn't looking for anything …just looking. The room was a snapshot in time from the
young girl's high school days. There were several photos of her
and Shelia. Gregory took a few of Catherine's pictures and put
them in his pocket, but not before massaging the bulge in his
pants. Catherine was a very attractive young lady… Still, Gregory
couldn't imagine cheating on his wife.

Gregory walked out of Catherine's bedroom and peeked his
head in the next bedroom to check on Nancy. She was still sound
asleep. He walked downstairs to start a light dinner for her because she would need to eat a little to keep up her strength.

Chapter 59

Gregory's second home was in the kitchen. He enjoyed cooking for his family when he had the chance. He looked around the kitchen to see what Nancy had to cook. She was right, she ate healthy. The bag of Doritos was probably Catherine's. He opened the bag and started to eat the chips, slapping his hands together when he was finished and washing his fingers under the warm water in the sink.

"Okay, it looks like it will be butternut squash soup," Gregory said out loud. He put a little sautéing oil in the pan and started to caramelize the shallots and garlic. After about ten minutes he added the sliced butternut squash and sautéed them, mixing constantly. Once the squash was softened Gregory added two cans of chicken broth and let the mixture simmer for about thirty minutes. He took a deep breath to let the aroma of the soup fill his soul. Homemade biscuits would add the needed touch to this meal, a meal to stick to your ribs. The biscuits went into the oven to rise and brown. He put the soft squash mixture into the blender and let it puree until it was silky and creamy. He poured half the mixture into a storage container and continued to blend the remaining soup. He transferred the soup to a bowl, with the golden biscuits and a dollop of sour cream. He washed the blender and dried it so as not leave a mess behind.

Gregory walked up the stairs to find Nancy watching television. "Hey, how are you feeling?"

"Just a little tired. The nap helped. What did you cook? It smells delicious."

"Butternut squash soup with an unhealthy biscuit."

"Are you going to have some?"

"No, I will keep you company while you eat."

"You will not. You will eat something." Nancy rose to leave the bed.

"Okay, I will fix me a plate and eat if you stay in bed."

Gregory poured his soup from the plastic container; the mixture for Nancy was disposed of when he washed the blender.

Gregory walked back upstairs and the two of them prayed together before sharing their meal. Nancy took a big bite of the warm, buttery biscuit that melted in her mouth. "This is wonderful. I know I didn't have any canned biscuits, so you must have made these from scratch."

"I did."

"And the soup, I know I didn't have squash soup in the cabinets, so you must have made that from scratch as well."

"What can I say, I am a man of many talents."

"Gregory, may I be blunt with you?"

"Sure."

Nancy rubbed her tired eyes.

"I stare into your eyes, and your soul seems to be troubled. You have a good heart and deep down you are a compassionate person, but your soul is empty." Nancy yawned; her eyes were not able to focus on Gregory.

"Nancy, are you okay?"

"Yes. With the deeds, you have done on earth, the Heavenly Father will not let you enter. There is a place for evil boys like yourself."

"Nancy, what are you saying?" Gregory was stunned.

"You know what I am saying. You are going to HELL for the deeds you have done on this earth. I can see right through you, and Satan has taken over your empty soul. You may take my life, but my soul will be with my Father."

Nancy closed her eyes and never woke. In the separate batch of soup Gregory made, he had crushed three Prozac pills and placed a pillow over her face. The kill was easy; she was lifeless and suffocated without a struggle. He liked Nancy and thought of her as a mother figure, but she had to be sacrificed to show Catherine he meant business. Gregory found the note that Catherine left for her mother and retrieved the phone number and address in NYC. He recorded the information in his phone and took his empty bowl of soup downstairs. He washed all the dishes and took the bag of Doritos with him.

Gregory got into the SUV and called the number Catherine left for her mother. He reached the voicemail of someone by the name of Samantha. "Hi, this message is for Catherine. You need to check on your mother." He hung up the phone and started the engine. As he drove, he called Amy to ask what was for dinner.

Chapter 80

The Megabus arrived at 7th Avenue and 27th Street in NYC. Catherine went into the nearest bodega and purchased a prepaid phone and immediately called Samantha. Catherine and Samantha had only been friends for a few months, but Catherine looked up to her as an older sister. Catherine had a client request that she go to La Perla and pick out lingerie for their date. He had left her an open credit line to pick out whatever she wanted. Samantha was the sales associate she worked with while finding what she needed for her date. She made Catherine feel at ease and that she could share anything with her. Over the next several months they had a girls' night where they caught up on their week's activity and just laughed.

The phone call went straight to voicemail and Catherine decided not to leave a message, but to head over to La Perla, where Samantha was probably working.

Chapter 61

The taxi pulled up in front of La Perla and Catherine got out and tipped the driver. The store was empty and Samantha was sipping champagne when Catherine entered.

"Hi, how are you," replied Samantha. "Catherine, is that you? What are you doing with the hideous wig on? Girl, come here."

Catherine walked over to Samantha, who snatched the wig off her head.

"I have been trying to call you. Why haven't you returned my phone calls?"

Catherine started to cry.

"What's wrong? Did something happen in Philly? I hate that God forsaken city. I lost the one person I love in that town and will never set foot there again. Enough about me—what's going on with you?"

Catherine took a deep breath, but only started to cry again.

"Here, here, Catherine. Let me get you a glass of champagne to calm your nerves."

Samantha went to the back of the store and brought out a champagne flute. She poured Catherine a glass.

Catherine reached for the drink and in three gulps the glass was empty.

"Damn, girl. What's going on with you? Let me pour you another glass, but slow down."

Samantha poured another glass of champagne and sat with Catherine until she was ready to speak.

"I went home to visit my mother and I contacted Stella to find out if there were any jobs for the weekend in Philly. I needed to earn extra money so that my mother could have a home health-care sitter stay with her during the day to make sure that she has three meals a day and takes her medication. Stella had a cancellation and I took the job. The night was going well until I accidently sent pictures of us to his wife. I think it was his wife but I am not sure because his mother showed up at the door and the two of them were having an argument. She came in and asked him how much I knew, which makes me think that he wasn't who he said he was. I think he was someone important and used the name Andy as an alias."

"Did you recognize him? Do you think he is an actor?"

"All I know is that he looked familiar, but I am not sure why. My friend Shelia sketched his features from my description, but we came up with nothing as well. Now someone is following me who doesn't want me to talk."

"Don't you think that is a little extreme, Catherine?"

"When I was in the apartment and the lady came by, she told Andy that because the pictures were sent they would have to kill me."

"Kill you?"

"I caught the first Megabus out of Philly to NYC. This guy wanted to get on the bus to talk to me."

"Okay, okay. Maybe you need to lie low for a while. You can

stay at my apartment for a few days to make sure that you are safe and you feel comfortable going back home."

"Thank you so much."

Catherine finished off her glass of champagne as Samantha handed her the apartment key.

"You need to go easy on that stuff. Go to the apartment and get some rest—you look like hell. We'll go to Chelsea Pier for dinner later."

"That sounds good." Catherine took a glance at herself in the mirror; the dark circles under her eyes and pale skin made her unrecognizable.

Catherine exited the store and hailed a cab with the brunette wig in her right hand.

Chapter 62

*B*rendon arrived at 425 West 14th Street and entered La Perla, on a mission to find sexy lingerie for Emily. Their anniversary was in two days and since he was in New York on business, it gave him a chance to pick up a special gift. Really, this would be a gift for him when he saw Emily in the beautiful and delicate piece of heaven. Brendon was in the middle of the store licking his lips as he imagined Emily in a G-string when his trance was interrupted by the sales associate.

"Can I help you?"

Brendon quickly said no; he was embarrassed and not sure if she saw that bulge in his pants had started to grow. She said her name was Samantha and she told him to let her know if he needed assistance. Brendon couldn't help but notice she was quite attractive.

Samantha stood five-foot-ten, with jet-black hair slightly pulled back and ruby red lips. She commanded the attention of all the men as they swooned over her striking facial features and long legs. Samantha had never settled on any particular guy until recently. Now, she was in an open relationship with Richard. The open relationship's true meaning was that Richard was married and he could see her whenever he wanted but she couldn't date anyone else. Richard rented the Chelsea apartment she lived in, not far from her part-time job at La Perla.

After Julia broke her heart in college Samantha was jaded on relationships and vowed never to let anyone break her heart again. So, every year or so Samantha moved on to a new relationship. Currently, she was tired of Richard and wanted something different. The customer in the store looked like he would fit the bill for her next conquest. He seemed as though he had a job of high importance, with his gray Brooks Brothers suit and a starched shirt. He was shopping in a high-end lingerie store, so he knew how to treat his lady. He had a high sexual appetite because he lost his composure while looking at lingerie. He may be able to keep up his stamina without taking the blue pill. *This is going to be too easy*, Samantha thought as she planned to lay on the charm.

Brendon brought his selections to the counter for checkout.

"Did you find everything okay?"

"Yes, I did."

"Is this purchase for a special occasion? I can wrap it for you."

"Please. It's our anniversary and I wanted to get my wife something special."

"Oh, that is nice. What size is she? Your sizes are across the board."

"I have no clue what size she is. I would think that she is a medium."

"What's your name?"

"My name is Brendon."

"I'm Samantha. Let's find the correct sizes you need. What's your wife's name?"

"Her name is Emily."

As he described his wife, Samantha felt her stomach churn

and hands moved to fists that she opened and closed in rage. She couldn't keep her composure and broke out in a sweat. Her mouth was dry and the words were difficult for her to form. *His whore of a wife stole Julia from me for nothing. Julia and Emily aren't even together. And I don't think Brendon is aware that my girlfriend loved his wife.*

Unless Emily had gained weight, Samantha knew exactly the sizes he needed. She ran through the store and collected the proper sizes for Brendon. Before reaching the sales counter, Samantha took a deep breath and regained her composure. She reached into her pocket for her daily dose of Prozac. She swallowed the pill and, when she reached the counter, washed it down with a bottle of Evian. Samantha approached Brendon with confidence and seduction. She told him she had his sizes and purposefully dropped her pen on the floor so she could bend over ever so gracefully with her hips in the air. Her short skirt barely covered her mid-thigh and when she bent over, her garter and stockings showed along with her ass. Samantha felt Brendon's eyes on her as she slowly stood up straight. She turned and gave him a shy look. Brendon licked his lips and rubbed the front of his pants, wanting to see and experience more.

Samantha cashed out the sale and gave Brendon her business card with her personal address. "If you want to see the city, you can come by my apartment and I will show you whatever you want to see."

"I may just do that. What time do you get off today?"

"Six thirty."

"Have a nice day, Samantha."

Samantha watched him as he left the store. It was only fair. Since Emily stole her partner, she would steal hers if only for one night.

Chapter 63

Samantha left work around 6:30 p.m., exhausted. She had flirted with all the male customers, the female ones too, looking for an opportunity to leave Richard. Somebody had to pay her bills. She thought the arrangement would be seeing Richard several times a month, but he wanted to cash in on the dividends he was paying upfront. She had to see him at least four days a week. As Samantha thought about her misery over the Richard situation, the doorman called to announce the arrival of Brendon Graham.

"Ms. Moore, you have a guest…Andy."

"I am sorry. I don't know anyone by the name of Andy."

Samantha moved toward the monitor to view her guest. It was Brendon.

"It is okay to send him up."

Samantha cracked the door so Brendon could enter without knocking. She was dressed in a negligee and high heel slippers with a fluffy feather on top.

Brendon exited the elevator and moved toward Samantha's apartment, smiling to see the door ajar.

Samantha emerged from the bedroom and gave Brendon a kiss on the cheek. "I am so glad that you made it."

"I would not have missed an opportunity to see you again."

"Would you like something to drink?"

"Scotch on the rocks."

Samantha went over to the bar and poured Brendon a scotch on the rocks while pouring herself a glass of chardonnay. Samantha added more wiggle to her step because she knew she had an audience. She handed Brendon his drink and kissed him on the lips. Brendon kissed Samantha's soft lips and pressed his penis against her as it swelled in his pants. Samantha caressed his penis to get him started. She touched him back and forth. Brendon did not object to how he was being touched by Samantha; in fact, he enjoyed confidence in a woman.

"Do you like what you see?"

"I liked what I saw at the store earlier. That is why I am here now."

Samantha rubbed her hand across the front of Brendon's pants and he grew harder with each touch. She took his jacket off while Brendon was unbuckling his belt and unzipping his pants. They fell to his ankle and he stepped out of them while holding on to her ass. Samantha led him to the bedroom and they both undressed themselves. They moved to the bed and started to have intercourse, with Brendon moving up and down on top of her. Their low moans showed that they were enjoying each other's company.

"Hello, Samantha, are you home?" yelled Catherine as she entered the apartment. She stopped in her tracks when she saw male pants in the living room. The door to the bedroom was cracked and Catherine saw Samantha having sex with a man. Catherine was intrigued and turned on by watching her friend have sex. She started to touch her breasts, which became erect with her touch. Samantha moved to straddle her lover; as he moved from the top to the bottom, Catherine caught a glimpse of him. *Samantha is having sex with Andy!* Did she know him? Catherine was confused and backed up from Samantha's bedroom door. She caught her breath, in awe that the person she had sex with and who was chasing her in the streets of Philly was in the apartment having sex with her friend.

Catherine went into the kitchen to get a glass of wine. She opened two cabinets before she found the red wine glasses. The half bottle of wine was sitting on the counter and Catherine reached for it to fill her wine glass. The light to the answering machine was flashing and Catherine hit play. The message came over loud and clear that her mother needed to be checked on. Catherine's gut instinct was that something had happened to her mother and the person leaving the message caused it. She imagined he had a connection to Andy, the guy Samantha was in bed with. Catherine played the message back a second time to make sure of what she heard and picked up the phone to find the number of the caller.

"Well, hello, Catherine," said the stranger on the other end.

"How do you know my name?"

"There isn't much we don't know about you."

"Who is we?"

"What you need to know is that your mother didn't go down without a fight."

"What do you mean?"

"You heard me; your mother didn't go down without a fight. You need to check on her estate."

Catherine trembled as she held the phone and couldn't imagine a world without her mother. "What have you done to my mother?"

"Catherine, I need to play the last card that I have. You need to come back to Philly to confront the situation with you and Andy. I need to make sure you don't take the information you know to the press."

"Why would I come to Philly? So, you can kill me? I heard the two of them saying that they wanted me dead. Okay, I will head back to Philly." Catherine had a change of heart. "What is your cell phone number so I can call you when I arrive?"

"I want you back by tomorrow. Can you handle that?"

"I will make it work."

Catherine was pacing back and forth in the small kitchen, trying to figure out how she would get out of this situation. Catherine searched for her phone, which was on the sofa, and moved toward Samantha's bedroom to take pictures of Andy. In the shadows, Catherine saw that Samantha had spotted her taking photos and was positioning herself so that Catherine could get a better angle of Andy with fewer pictures of herself.

Samantha went in for the third round, which caused Andy to move back on top of his lover. Catherine moved from photos to videoing the sexual encounter between Samantha and Andy. After several minutes of documenting the events, Catherine went to her bedroom and sent a text message to the mystery man on the phone with the caption, "Don't fuck with me." After several minutes where she didn't hear back from the mystery man, she turned her phone on Do Not Disturb and fell asleep.

Gregory heard the distracting noise the phone made when he received a new text message. He read the message from Catherine and was impressed with the quality of the video she sent and the tone of the text message. Catherine would have to die but he needed time to find her. She was proving to be a thorn in his side and he needed to tie up this loose end soon before she created more damage. Gregory immediately called Brendon's cell, which went straight to voicemail. "Man, pick up the damn phone. We have a problem with Catherine. Call me ASAP."

Chapter 64

Brendon slept beside Samantha until the wee hours of the morning and reached for his iPhone to see the exact time. It was 4:00 and Brendon had several text messages from Gregory. All five messages essentially said that his situation had been compromised and to contact Gregory ASAP. The next text message told Brendon to go to his email to review a video. Brendon clicked the link to the video embedded in his email. The video clearly showed Brendon having sex with Samantha.

"But who would do something like this?"

Brendon looked around the room and couldn't believe he was in another situation that would cause embarrassment to his family. "Why do I keep causing heartache to those I love the most?"

Brendon picked up each piece of clothing scattered around the room and walked toward the bathroom. The door leading to the second bathroom was slightly open. Brendon stood in the doorway and peered at the beautiful young lady sleeping in nothing but a tank top and panties. Brendon grew hard staring at the beautiful blonde. He dropped his clothes so he could have both hands to take care of his arousal. The blonde stirred and turned her face toward the door. Brendon looked down at his arousal and caressed it back and forth. He let his body feel the pleasure of the short but smooth strokes. He looked up and stumbled back…he was staring at Catherine's peaceful face. He rushed to the bathroom to get dressed. Before he put a piece of clothing on, he hit speed dial and called Gregory.

"Where the hell are you, man? I have sent you numerous texts and a video that was taken of you."

"Gregory, I am in big trouble. I am still at Samantha's apartment, a girl I met yesterday, but that's not the biggest problem we have."

"No, you don't think that is huge?"

"The girl that got away, Catherine, she is here. She took the pictures and the video. They are both trying to frame me."

"What? Catherine is at the apartment too. How do you know?"

"I was just staring at her sleeping."

"Shit, where are you? Text me the address." Gregory threw the coffee he was drinking in the trash and jogged down the block to his SUV. He eased out of the parking space onto the busy street toward Chelsea.

Chapter 65

Gregory found the nearest parking space to the address that Brendon texted him and walked toward the fancy building with his sunglasses on and a baseball cap tightly on his head. He texted Brendon to alert the doorman to send him straight up.

"Good morning, I am here to see Samantha."

"Yes, sir," said Jake, the doorman. "Your name is on the list." He escorted Gregory to the elevator and pushed the button for the eleventh floor. "Good day, sir."

"Thanks."

Gregory exited the elevator and quietly entered the apartment that Brendon left unlocked. Brendon popped his head out of the bathroom and sighed in relief when he saw Gregory, who placed his index finger to his lips, indicating for Brendon not to make a sound. He looked around the room and walked toward the kitchen with two dish towels and neatly folded both. He pulled the bottle of chloroform out of his back pocket and soaked both rags with the liquid that smelled faintly of rotting fruit.

In a low whisper, he said to Brendon, "You place the rag over Samantha's nose and mouth and hold it there until I come back to the room. Where is Catherine? I want to take care of that bitch myself."

"She is in the room near the bathroom, over there."

They took their towels to the rooms where the women were sleeping. Gregory entered Catherine's room and walked toward the bed.

"Catherine, wake up." He shook her shoulder a couple of times and she opened her eyes to the man who was chasing her around Center City and who probably killed her mother. He had her shoulders pinned down so she could no longer move. The dish towel was covering her nose and mouth. She felt her body losing control of her muscles, she started to relax, and her breathing became labored. Gregory kept one hand on the cloth and reached in his left sock for one of the syringes of valium. Catherine's body grew limp and he removed the cloth from her face before injecting the liquid magic in between the big and second toes of her left foot. He squeezed the plunger and the needle emptied. "You fucked with the wrong man." Gregory left Catherine's body on the bed without looking back. He didn't care about her, just about getting the work done for Kyndall.

Gregory entered Samantha's room and found Brendon kneeling on the floor with the towel on his lover's face. She probably succumbed to death five minutes earlier, but Gregory didn't work off assumptions. He needed to know without a shadow of a doubt that Samantha was dead. He bent at the waist and found the last of the needles and injected it in the same place as he did Catherine, right between the toes. Gregory removed the needle and headed for the kitchen to place both needles in a plastic grocery store bag and shove them into his pocket. He looked around the room for the thermostat and adjusted the temperature to sixty-eight degrees with his gloved hand.

Gregory then walked toward the bathroom and saw Brendon still kneeling beside Samantha's body.

"It's okay, she's dead. You can remove the cloth. As a matter of fact, give it to me."

Brendon moved the cloth he was holding in his right hand and wiped the tears forming on his cheek with his left hand.

"The cloth, Brendon." Gregory rolled his eyes in Brendon's direction.

Brendon handed the cloth to Gregory, who put it in the bag along with the other supplies used to kill both witnesses. "Brendon, I know this kind of stuff that I do is hard for you to handle, but we need to be out of here within the next five minutes. I need you to go in the kitchen and load the dishwasher to wash any evidence from the glasses that were in the sink. Find any cleaner and wipe down every place in the kitchen you might have touched. I will start in the bathroom. Yell when you are done."

Brendon didn't move, nor did he respond.

Gregory moved closer to Brendon and shook his shoulders. "Man, snap out of it." Brendon moved his head in the direction of the voice, which now was unrecognizable. "Brendon, are you okay?" Brendon forced his eyes to focus on the person speaking the words. The image of Gregory was now before him as he slowly came back to reality. He looked at the body and back at Gregory and then understood what just happened. He fell and started a backward crawl away from the body.

"Hey, man, let me help you up." Gregory extended his right hand to Brendon, who reached for it to help him to his feet. "Will you clean the kitchen and put the dishes in the dishwasher?"

"Sure."

"I will start on the bathroom."

The two cleaned in silence and Gregory moved to Catherine's room. He picked up the chloroform-soaked cloth and placed it in the plastic bag. Gregory and Brendon met in Samantha's room and wiped everything down, including the headboard.

"Did you use a condom?"

"Yeah."

"Did you flush?"

"Of course."

"Where is the wrapper? I didn't see it in the bathroom trash and there isn't a trash can in here." Brendon looked around the room, under the bed, and nothing.

"Shit. I don't know where it is."

The sound of the door unlocking forced them both to turn their attention away from the dead body.

"Keep looking for the wrapper and I will take care of whoever is at the front door." Gregory ran toward the door, picking up a glass vase as he took his position behind it.

The door slowly opened. "Hello, Samantha, this is Jake. Mr. Richard wanted me to check on you because you weren't answering your phone." Two more steps and Jake was totally in the apartment, closing the door behind him. With two arms raised above his head, Gregory smashed the vase on the doorman's head, shattering it into tiny pieces. The body hit the floor hard and Jake was unconscious. Gregory rummaged through his pocket for his driver's license and placed it in his back pocket.

"Brendon, we've got to go. Do you have it?"

"Yeah, it was under the bed."

"Okay, let's go."

Gregory and Brendon stepped over Jake's body as Gregory opened the door with his gloved hand. Brendon moved in the direction of the elevator, but Gregory motioned toward the stairwell. They descended the stairs in silence and once they got to the first floor, Gregory gave Brendon his cap and sunglasses and told him where the car was. He gave him the keys to the SUV. Gregory pulled the hoodie on his head and stopped at the front desk, where he hit various keys and entered codes and erased the video from the night before and that morning. Gregory exited the building and entered the SUV, which Brendon had parked, waiting for him outside of the apartment. Brendon sped off down the street in the direction of the George Washington Bridge and back to Philadelphia.

Chapter 88

"Julia, hi, this is Emily. How are you? It has been quite a while since the two of us have spoken."

"Hey, Em, thank you for returning my phone call. I wasn't sure if I would hear from you. It's been many years since I heard from you, and when your mother and I spoke the other day, I didn't think that you would want to speak with me."

Emily paused for a moment to collect her thoughts, but also to digest the new Julia she was experiencing, who was more insecure and hiding behind the image society had shaped for her. Emily was saddened that the person she looked up to, who exhibited confidence and commanded the attention of others, had succumbed to settling for a typical life.

"Oh, no, Julia. I have had so much on my plate lately that I didn't have the opportunity to return your call. Besides, I didn't want to complicate your life with my family's efforts to get Brendon elected as President of the United States."

Emily thought about the polite conversation they were having and wanted the questions in her head answered, so she just blurted out what was on her mind. "Julia, you hurt me when we were in college. We were at the bar to celebrate your graduation and when I came back from the restroom I saw you kissing Samantha. I thought we were going to start a life together."

"Emily, that night I had all intentions of asking you to be in a relationship, but Samantha came up and we did kiss. Shortly after you left, I broke up with her because I loved you."

Emily felt embarrassed; she had assumed that Julia didn't care about her. She was relieved that the love between the two of them was real. "Julia, I had no idea that you broke up with Samantha. I left with Brendon that night because I was hurt and needed to feel loved and I knew he cared for me. It was that night that I decided to start a life with him and leave what I thought we had behind. I was always haunted that I didn't follow the right path. You were the one I should have been with. Don't get me wrong, I love Brendon and the life we created, but I live every day thinking about what if we were together. What would our life be like if we had pursued our love?"

"I don't know how to answer that question other than to say we lived the life that we were supposed to live. I have no regrets and I am comfortable with the life that my husband and I have. I would not trade it for anything in the world. For you to move on, you need to find some closure; you need to accept who you are and the road that you have traveled."

"I can't wait to see you in a couple of weeks."

"Me too; I will talk to you soon." They ended the call feeling as though they had closure to the past.

earl stirred in her bed. The noise from the front of the house disrupted her sleep. *Bam, bam, bam.* The knocker on the front door echoed throughout the house, eventually waking both Emily and Pearl.

Emily glanced at the clock on Brendon's side of the bed, which read 2:00 a.m. No good news was delivered at that hour. Emily panicked and reached for her phone, needing to find out if her mother had an emergency. Nothing—no messages from anyone. Her nerves started to calm as she hurried to find her robe and slippers and walked by Brendon, lying next to her. She breathed a sigh of relief. *He wasn't involved in any scandals…at least not tonight.*

Ms. Pearl reached the door before Emily reached the bottom of the stairs. "Hello, who is it?"

"Mrs. Graham, this is State Trooper Quincy Davidson."

Pearl opened the door slightly. "Can I see your badge?" Black-on-black crimes in her neighborhood had made her skeptical of the police and their level of helpfulness with African Americans. Pearl knew the police weren't coming after her, but she wanted everyone to understand that she was an upstanding individual in the community.

Pearl carefully opened the door after the trooper proved his identity. It was important not to protect herself, but the reputation of the Grahams. No one would tarnish their image while she was around.

"Ma'am, I am sorry to wake you in the middle of the night but is Mr. or Mrs. Graham home?" asked Trooper Davidson.

Emily appeared from behind Pearl. "I am Mrs. Graham."

"There has been an accident and we need you to come to the hospital. Julia Banks' son and husband were admitted to the hospital and we need to escort you there. It is our understanding that she was on her way to visit you when she and her family were hit by a drunk driver."

"Officer, give me a minute. I need to change."

Emily ran up the stairs and changed into sweat pants and a sweat shirt. She hurried back downstairs to be escorted to the hospital by Trooper Davidson.

They arrived at the hospital to find Julia in the waiting area, pacing back and forth.

"Hi Emily; it is so good to see you."

"Hi Julia. I wish we were seeing each other under different circumstances. How is your family?"

"My husband and son have both been admitted. Stanley needs a blood transfusion, but his blood type is so rare, there isn't a match."

"I'm not sure of my blood type but I am willing to find out if I am a match."

"I have given blood, but I am not a match. I would not think either my husband and I are matches because Stanley is adopted. Either way my husband is giving blood to find out if he is a match."

"Julia, I don't think that I have met your husband. I would like to meet him. Where is he?"

"Oh, Emily, I thought I told you that I married Dave Banks, the psychology teacher from Temple. He's in examination room three getting stitches."

Out of nowhere Emily raised her hand and slapped Julia across the face. "How could you?" The sting of the slap turned Julia's head to the right and left an imprint of Emily's hand on Julia's face.

Julia rubbed her face, but her pride hurt more than anything. Why would the love of her life slap her? "Emily, what's going on?"

"Dave is the one who raped me while at Temple and I got pregnant. I gave my baby up for adoption because Brendon and I were too young to care for a baby. His name was Ian."

"I never knew any of this, but I don't believe that Dave raped you. He is a gentle soul who could never harm or inflict pain on anyone."

"Julia, I know this is hard to believe, but I was in our dorm room expecting Brendon. Dave came up behind me and had sex with me. I didn't know it wasn't Brendon. He took advantage of me. I don't understand why you would be with someone so cruel. How can you love someone who violated me? I thought you loved me? You are not the person I thought you were."

"Emily, I did not know. Dave never told me that he had sex with you and the two of you had a son. Did he know you were pregnant?"

"He knew he raped me. I saw him months later and he avoided eye contact with me, but smiled as we passed each other in the hallway."

"Emily, it's not that I don't believe you, but this just doesn't seem like something Dave would do."

"Just know that I am getting my blood tested, not for you or that bastard Dave but for Stanley, your innocent son." Emily left Julia's presence in a huff and walked toward the nurses' station.

The nurse came back with the results of the blood tests from

Julia, Dave, and Emily, and it turned out that Dave and Emily were the perfect match to donate blood for Stanley. Julia received the news and acknowledged what Emily was saying to her was the truth. Dave and Emily had sexual relations and conceived a child together. Why didn't Dave reveal his love for Emily? Did he use her to get close to Emily? Julia could not think straight about the relationship she had with Dave. There were many unanswered questions swirling around in her mind. She did recall Dave leaving their dorm room and exiting the stairs.

Why would an instructor be in the dorms and coming from the direction of our room? The day I bumped into Dave when I was leaving campus…was it a coincidence? How did he get my cell number to call me after graduation? I was never in any of his classes, so there was no need for him to have my number. Julia felt light-headed and the room started to spin. She backed up against the wall to brace herself from an inevitable fall. Emily grabbed Julia by the arm and walked with her to the closest chair in the waiting area.

The nurse turned to Emily with a direct question that brought everything to light about the dark secret Dave had kept from his precious wife all these years. "Mrs. Banks, are you and your husband ready to give blood?"

"She's Mrs. Banks. I am Mrs. Graham, and yes, I am ready to give blood."

"Oh, I am sorry for the mix-up." The nurse looked at both women, feeling the pain of them both. She knew what it was like for deception to ruin the lives of bystanders. Her father, as the song went, was a rolling stone. She had three sisters and two brothers she knew nothing about until her father's funeral last spring. One of her brothers she had dated two years prior. She dodged that bullet and shook her head, not at the awkward situation before her but at her own life. Everyone had a story to tell or a story they never wanted anyone to ever know. "Follow me" was the only response she had for the group.

The doctor stitching up Dave exited the room, closing the door behind him. Julia approached him. "Is Dave okay?"

The doctor smiled. "He was banged up a little and the stitches will absorb into his skin within a few weeks. If he has any complications, please come back to see me."

Julia nodded and thanked the doctor. She carefully opened the door to the exam room.

"Hi, honey. I am all better, just like new."

"Did you rape Emily?"

Dave's eyes were fixed to the floor as the question about Emily was asked, and he smiled with a spark of lust in his eyes. "Be careful what you ask. Do you really want to know the answer to that question?"

"Yes, I do."

"Yes, I had sex with Emily."

"So it is true that you raped her."

"I didn't rape her. She wanted it. She wanted me. I could see it in her eyes every time she came to class with those short skirts and yoga pants where you can see the indentation of every body part. In my defense, she seduced me."

"You sick SOB. I confessed my love for Emily to you and all the while you were lusting after her. You knew I loved her. Why didn't you tell me that you loved her too?"

"Now what would have been the fun in that? You were distraught after Emily left you for that fellow and couldn't bear to move on. It was my duty as a professional to help you. You have to agree that I picked up the pieces and put you back together again, but little did I know that you would live your entire life wanting someone you could never have."

"Well, I could say the same for you too."

"But on the contrary, I had Emily in a way that you will never know," said Dave with a grin that showed all his pearly white teeth.

"You disgust me."

"Well, I would be hurt if that was the first time I heard that comment." Dave eased off the examination table and adjusted his shirt and pants. Even though he was an older man, he still paid extra care to his grooming and thought of himself as a ladies' man.

"Did you know that you and Emily are a perfect match to donate blood to Stanley? Stanley is the son who you and Emily created from the rape."

Dave was genuinely stunned by the news of Stanley as his natural son. Life had a way of throwing curve balls, but this news changed Dave's outlook. He had never had children with his first wife, and he and Julia could not conceive. They never went to a specialist; just wanted to let nature take its course. Dave did love Julia and it didn't matter if they had children or not; however, the news of him having a son made his chest puff out. He was a proud father, even though Stanley had emotional issues. "Julia, nothing you can say will ruin the news that I have a son. I am overjoyed." Dave did a two-step as though he was hearing music.

The knock on the door brought the dancing to a halt. Julia yelled, "Come in!" She needed the distraction. Nurse Gwendolyn appeared from around the door. "Hi, I wanted to know if Mr. Banks was ready to give blood. Mrs. Banks, I mean Mrs. Graham just gave blood and is resting. Are you ready?"

"Where is Emily?" Dave asked.

"Mr. Banks, as I mentioned, she is resting after giving blood."

"Can I see her?"

"She requested not to see anyone. If you will follow me, we can begin the procedure."

After all these years, Emily didn't want to see Dave either. He had been with many women and married twice, but Emily was his only true love. Dave shuffled down the hall after the nurse; he couldn't focus on Emily now. He needed to give the blood that his son needed to fight for his life. When Stanley recovered, Dave vowed to make up for lost time. Maybe one day the three of them could be a family.

Chapter 68

*I*t had been years since Kyndall drove down the familiar street. The houses looked smaller and more weather worn. The chipped paint and unkempt lawns told the story of a community neglected by its owners. Caught up in her thoughts, Kyndall braked hard to avoid darting through the stop sign. She surveyed the intersection for oncoming traffic. An older woman with silver hair steadied herself with a metal can as she placed her hand on a mailbox. No door, just the metal box on a stand, exposing all its contents. *What happened to the door? Why didn't she ever get the door fixed?* The hurried honk of the driver in the blue Chevy brought Kyndall's thoughts back to the intersection. She removed her sunglasses and glared at the driver from her rearview mirror. The driver put his car in reverse and pulled around the sleek black Mercedes, eyeballing Kyndall as he sped past her, giving her his middle finger as he plowed through the stop sign. Kyndall, who was always up for a challenge, revved her engine to chase her mark.

In her peripheral vision, an object appeared on her right and landed with a bounce in the grass in front of her car. The two giggling children darted into the street, which caused Kyndall to strike her brake with the entire weight of her body. "Get out of the street! Where are your parents?" she yelled as she crept through the stop sign, losing the blue Chevy.

As Kyndall continued to drive down the street, the children disappeared in the distance as she got closer to the reason she was strolling down memory lane in this dilapidated neighborhood. She needed to pay a visit to confront the one person she thought over the years had grown to be one of her closest friends, as close as anyone could get to Kyndall's steel heart. The family events—holidays, birthdays, and other special occasions—helped the two of them get to know and understand each other better. *I knew all those years ago, Doris may not have agreed with my negotiation tactics but she needed me at the time and I needed her as well. Doris helped me craft my plan for Brendon's future; he wouldn't have gotten this far without her.*

Kyndall turned her left blinker on and pulled into Doris's driveway. She sat in her car for several minutes, not moving, but dreading the conversation she had to have with Doris. Kyndall didn't have a lot of friends and to classify Doris as a friend, Kyndall felt a sharp pain that someone in her inner circle had betrayed her. *Why is she making me do this to her? I told Doris when I gave her the money to save the house from foreclosure, she needed to uphold her end of the deal, but she couldn't even do that. Oh, she convinced Emily to change her feelings for Julia and Brendon, but after all these years Doris grew a conscience.*

Doris had pissed her off when she initiated the reconciliation between Julia and Emily. Kyndall had asked herself, "What for?" Both Julia and Emily had moved on with their lives. "Now, the turmoil of all our lives is exposed for people to gawk at the future first family. The world knows that Dave raped Emily, which resulted in the birth of that demon-possessed boy of hers, Stanley. Julia and Emily are barely speaking to one another now because Emily can't get over the fact that Julia married the person who assaulted her." Kyndall was speaking out loud, but no one heard her. She was in the car, alone. The veins in her forehead were visible and pronounced as she rubbed her temples with both hands, round and round, forward and backward. Kyndall pulled the latch of the door while thinking, *I had everyone's life under control, until Doris reached out to Julia and my world turned to ruin with just one phone call."*

When the black Mercedes pulled in the driveway, Doris peeked her head out the front door. She had been expecting this visit from Kyndall for some time, and lived on edge, not knowing when she or that gut-twisting Gregory would be called upon to "scare" her. Doris knew when she reached out to Julia, she had betrayed Kyndall's trust. She shook her head and stood tall with her head high, telling herself not to be a coward because the reaper was there to call her debt to be paid. *If I must die, I want my conscience to be clear that I did the right thing in the end. I let Julia and Emily choose how they wanted to shape the rest of their lives.*

Doris flung the door open and stood on the porch, waving to Kyndall, in her way, to let her know she was ready to bear any punishment she was about to endure. Doris slowly whispered to herself, "I have made peace with my actions. Dear Lord, have mercy on my soul."

Kyndall gave Doris a half smile and walked over to the passenger side of the car, unlocked the door, and reached into the glove box for her Smith and Wesson. She slid the gun into her handbag and close it tightly. *What a shame*, Kyndall thought as she closed the door and locked it.

Doris greeted Kyndall with a hug and kiss on the cheek. "Hi Kyndall, how are you?"

Kyndall pulled back from Doris's embrace. "I am well and you?"

Doris eyed Kyndall and saw she was strictly business. She got straight to the point. "I wish your visit was under different conditions."

"Me too; I am going to cut to the chase. You know I am not big on beating around the bush."

"You definitely can be direct when you want to be."

"Why, after all these years, did you decide to contact Julia? You knew nothing good would come from you unraveling what took me so long to put together."

"I know" was the only response Doris could give. Emily's life was a bigger mess than before. Even though Doris was prepared to accept her part in all the commotion, a tear streamed down her cheek as she wrestled with the thought that she would never see her dear Emily again.

While Doris was deep in thought, Kyndall reached for the gun in her purse. She needed to get this over with, and she had plans for lunch with Wellington.

Doris focused her attention back on Kyndall and saw her pull a gun out of her purse. Doris glided to the right and quickly opened the end table drawer while keeping an eye on Kyndall; she blindly used her hand to feel for the knife. The handle fit like a glove in her arthritic hand. Expeditiously, Doris brought the knifed hand toward Kyndall's chest. Kyndall moved to the right and the knife nicked her on the left arm. She immediately grabbed her arm in pain while dropping her purse, all the contents spilling out over the floor. However, she still managed to keep the gun in her right hand and squeezed the trigger to hit her target on the right shoulder. *Bang!* The knife Doris was holding fell to the floor. Doris pushed Kyndall against the wall with the gun sliding under the sofa. Both their eyes moved from the gun under the chair to the knife within inches of them both. When they dived on the floor, Doris found the knife, but Kyndall's main objective was to locate the gun, which she managed to do by crawling on her hands and knees toward the sofa. Doris's hand found the steel knife with the black handle with the tip of her fingers and pulled in both her hands to come down hard on her prey. Kyndall turned the gun around and hit Doris with the butt of the gun over her head. Doris fell to the ground motionless. Kyndall crawled toward her cell phone and dialed 911.

"Hello, what's your emergency?"

Kyndall screamed, "She's trying to kill me! Please hurry."

"Ma'am, what's your name and who is trying to kill you?"

Kyndall ignored the questions and only gave the operator the address. She refused to give her name on a recorded telephone line. "Please hurry," she repeated before hanging up the phone. Kyndall raised the gun with a steady hand, stood over Doris's body, and shot her once in the chest. Blood oozed out onto the floor as Kyndall took her shirt tail and wiped her prints from the gun. She placed it in Doris's hand and aimed for her thigh. "Shit, that hurts," screamed Kyndall. She carefully let the gun fall to the ground near Doris to purposefully contaminate the evidence. In the distance, she heard the ambulance sirens and waited to be rescued as she knew Doris was already dead.